The Secret Attic

"This is so strange," whispered Cricket, breaking the silence. "I feel like . . . like there's something up here."

"You mean a treasure?" Meg said, remembering what she'd been thinking earlier about finding an old baseball card collection. Looking at the jumble of old boxes and trunks that surrounded them, it certainly seemed possible.

"Maybe that," Cricket murmured. "Or maybe something else. Something bigger. I know you don't believe in these things. But I really do have a feeling that there's something up here that could change our lives!"

Meg and the Secret Scrapbook

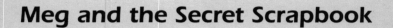

Meg and the Secret Scrapbook

Susan Meyers

Troll Associates

For Jocie and Jessica, who will always be friends

Chapter

Scared! That's what Meg Kelly was. Her heart was pounding, the palms of her hands pressed against the back seat of the car were sweating, and her breakfast of scrambled eggs and toast seemed dangerously close to moving from her stomach to her throat.

This is stupid, she told herself as her mother pulled the car to a halt in front of Redwood Grove Elementary School. The bell was ringing and a few last minute stragglers were racing up the steps. So what if I'm going to an all new school, in an all new town, where I don't know a single, solitary soul. So what if I never have another friend as long as I live. So what if I'm never invited to another sleepover. So what if—

"Meg, are you going to just sit there?" Her mother had already gotten out of the car, opened the back door, and released Kevin, Meg's four-and-a-half-year-old brother, from his seat belt. "Come on. We have to get you registered before I can take Kevin to nursery school."

"Why can't I go here?" said Kevin, jumping out of the car. "This looks like a good school."

"It is," said Mrs. Kelly, as Meg forced herself to climb out after him. "But the school you're going to is good, too." She paused and took a deep breath. "Mmm. Smell that air," she said. She put her hand on Meg's shoulder, as though she thought Meg might bolt and run like a frightened pony, and guided her toward the school. "You won't find anything like that in Los Angeles."

Meg had to admit she was right. The air in Redwood Grove was crisp and clear, with a scent of pine and redwood mingled with eucalyptus. And the air wasn't the only difference.

Los Angeles, where Meg had lived her entire life, was an enormous, sprawling city with tall buildings, huge shopping malls, freeways, and streets that were crowded with cars. Redwood Grove, where her mother had grown up and her grandparents still lived, was tiny by comparison. There were no department stores, no bowling alleys, no big movie complexes. Just a small downtown with pretty little shops and lots of houses nestled into the hills. The city of San Francisco was nearby, but even that was small compared to Los Angeles.

"You're going to love living in Redwood Grove," Meg's mother had said when she told Meg they were moving. That was a month ago when she'd gotten a job at a computer software company near Redwood Grove. She'd had to speak loudly because Meg had stormed into her room and slammed the door. "You've always liked visiting Grandma and Grandpa and now we'll actually be living with them, at least until I find us a place of our own. You can sleep in my old room. Maybe you can even get a kitten."

Meg knew a bribe when she heard one. She also knew she was being selfish. Her mother's work was important. Ever since her dad had died, just before Kevin was born, her mother had been the sole support of their family. But Meg couldn't help herself. Even the thought of a kitten—which she couldn't have in their no-pets apartment in Los Angeles—even the thought of living in her grandparents' big old house in the redwoods, of sleeping in her mother's old room, couldn't make up for leaving everything and everyone she'd ever known!

She was not going to think about that now, though. If she did, she was likely to lose all the courage she had. She was likely to forget all the things she'd been telling herself about how having friends didn't matter. She was likely, in fact, to burst into tears right in front of everyone at Redwood Grove Elementary School. And what kind of a start would that be?

"Come on, Kevin!" she said fiercely, slipping out of her mother's grasp. "Let's not crawl like turtles. I'll race you up the steps!"

Running was a good way to make herself feel better, but a bad way to enter a school office. Ms. Uchida, the secretary for Redwood Grove Elementary, frowned when Meg and Kevin burst through the doorway. Luckily, Mrs. Kelly wasn't far behind. She quickly calmed Kevin down, introduced herself and Meg, and began filling out the registration forms that Ms. Uchida handed her.

Meg caught her breath. So far, so good, she thought. Her breakfast was still in her stomach and her heart was probably just pounding from running. Now if I can just get Mom to clear out fast without a lot of hugs and kisses . . .

The school office was a lot like the one at her old school, Westside Elementary. There were lots of pictures and posters and a bulletin board full of announcements. Behind the counter that ran the length of the office, a woman was busily tapping at the keyboard of a computer, another woman was feeding papers into a copy machine, and a custodian was washing the windows that overlooked the front lawn. A boy with a bloody nose was sprawled out on a chair, his head tipped back, probably waiting for the nurse.

Kevin took one look at the boy and began tugging at his mother's skirt. "I want to go," he announced loudly. "I don't like this school. I like my school. Grandma says they've got rabbits there. I want to see rabbits. Do you think they got rabbits at this school, Meg?"

" 'Have,' Kevin. It's 'do they *have* rabbits,'" Meg corrected him. And all at once she felt jealous. Not of

Kevin exactly, but of how easy things were for him. All he'd have to do at nursery school was play in the sandbox, paint big messy pictures, and cuddle a bunch of sweet little rabbits. He wouldn't have to worry about catching up to the rest of the class in math, or wearing the right clothes, or finding someone to eat lunch with. Of course, he'd have to make friends. But even that was different when you were little.

"As a matter of fact, we do have rabbits here," said Ms. Uchida, smiling at Kevin from behind the front desk. "Maybe you'll see them when you come to kindergarten next year."

"That's right," agreed Mrs. Kelly, finishing the registration form and prying Kevin's hand from her skirt. "There are going to be lots of rabbits in your life, Kevin. Now, Meg, are you sure you're all right? You've got your lunch money?"

"Yes, Mom." Meg groaned, fighting down the lump that was rising in her throat. "And my shoelaces are tied and I've got a Kleenex in my pocket. Now go before Kevin wets his pants!"

"All right, Meg. No need to snap," said Mrs. Kelly, as Kevin started blustering about being too big a boy to wet his pants. "I'm sure you'll do fine. And remember, since I don't have to start my job until tomorrow, we can go clothes shopping after school today. We'll go to Baylor's, if that's still the place." She looked inquiringly at Ms. Uchida.

"Oh, it is," replied the secretary. "Lots of the girls

get their clothes there. I think they're having a sale this week."

She smiled at Meg. Was it with pity? Was the flowered dress with the crocheted vest, which was just right for her old school, totally wrong for Redwood Grove? Meg had a sinking feeling it was.

"Good," said Mrs. Kelly. "A sale is just what we need. I'll meet you right outside as soon as school's over, Meg," she said, smiling brightly—too brightly. "Can't wait to hear about your day." Then, almost before Meg realized it—and without any hugs and kisses at all!—she and Kevin were gone.

"Have a seat, dear," said Ms. Uchida kindly. "I'll phone Mr. Crockett's room and have him send someone to get you. And don't worry. School started just a week ago, so you haven't missed much. You'll like Mr. Crockett. He's one of our best fifth grade teachers."

Meg nodded, scarcely hearing what she said. She sank down on a chair across from the boy with the bloody nose. He was younger than she was, which was good. She didn't want to risk having someone in her own grade, someone she might run into on the play yard or in the cafeteria, witness her breakdown!

Keep up your courage. She repeated the words under her breath. They came from a book she'd read about a pioneer girl named Sarah Noble who'd had to trek through the snowy wilderness all by herself. The wolves were howling and the wind was whistling and the only thing that kept Sarah going was saying, *Keep*

up your courage, Sarah Noble. Keep up your courage.
If it worked for her, it might work for me, Meg figured, even if my name isn't Sarah Noble.

She slipped her hand into the pocket of her dress and fingered the tiny teddy bear that she'd hidden there this morning. Jenny Snyder, her best friend in all the world, had given it to her before she left Los Angeles. "It's so you won't forget me," Jenny had said, pressing the bear into Meg's hand. "All you have to do is look at its goofy face and you'll remember all the goofy things we did together."

Meg swallowed hard. She knew it was dangerous to think about Jenny now, but she couldn't help herself. She ran her fingers over the teddy bear's smiling face, its soft ears, its plump tummy. She pictured the big heart Jenny had drawn on its T-shirt and the words she had written inside—*Always Friends.*

Just as the lump in her throat got too large and her eyes seemed dangerously hot, Meg thought of her plan. Immediately she felt better. That's the way it had been ever since she thought it up. When things got really rough, all she had to do was remember the advertisement she'd found on one of the sheets of newspaper her mother was using to pack dishes. The top of the ad showed a picture of a sleek jet plane flying high above the clouds. Beneath it, in bold black print, it said:

$99 ROUND TRIP
LOS ANGELES—SAN FRANCISCO

Meg hadn't said anything then, but when her mother wasn't looking, she'd taken the paper, folded it up, and stuffed it into the box where she kept the stationery she planned to use for writing to Jenny.

Ninety-nine dollars was a lot of money. More money than Meg had ever had in her life. But if somehow she could get it, she would fly to Los Angeles and move in with Jenny. I could sleep in her upper bunk, she thought, and walk to Westside School with her every day. I wouldn't be any trouble. I'd make my bed, help with the dishes, wash my own clothes.

Of course, she thought, Mom and Kevin would miss her. But the ticket was round-trip. She could come back to Redwood Grove. Maybe for Christmas.

"Well, will you look at that!"

Meg jumped. She'd been thinking so hard about Jenny and the airplane ticket that she'd almost forgotten where she was. She saw the custodian staring out the window at a sleek black car—a limousine!—that had just come to a stop in front of the school. A man dressed in a uniform got out of the driver's side. He started to walk around the car, but before he could reach the other side, the back door opened and a girl leaped out. She looked about Meg's age, but there the resemblance stopped. Meg didn't have long, tawny blond hair, she didn't look like a fashion model, and she certainly wasn't wearing sleek black jeans, short red boots, and a suede jacket the color of toffee.

The girl dashed up the steps to the school and burst into the office, an anxious expression on her face. Ms. Uchida glanced at the clock on the wall and frowned. "Do you have a late note?" she asked.

"No, but I'll bring it tomorrow, I promise," the girl replied, her cheeks turning red. "I missed the bus, so the chauffeur . . . I mean, I came in the car," she stammered, her cheeks turning even redder.

"All right, run along then," said Ms. Uchida. "But be sure to bring that note tomorrow. We need it for our records."

"Oh, I will. *Merci* . . . I mean, thank you." The girl bobbed her head in what looked like a bow. And then, barely glancing at Meg, she dashed out the office door and was gone.

The custodian murmured something about how the town was changing. Meg sank back in her chair and stared at her feet, which were *not* encased in red leather boots. What kind of school was this anyway? Mom had said Redwood Grove was going to be a simpler place to live than Los Angeles, with down-to-earth values. She hadn't said anything about kids coming to school in limousines and wearing toffee-colored suede jackets. If that's the way it is around here, Meg thought, I'm sunk!

"Are you the new girl?"

For the second time, a voice startled Meg out of her thoughts. She took her eyes off her feet and looked up to see a skinny girl with curly red hair—just about the

17

reddest Meg had ever seen—and a friendly face. Her eyes were blue with pale gold lashes and zillions of freckles covered her cheeks.

"I'm Cricket," the girl introduced herself. "Like the bug. It's Catherine, really—Catherine Connors—but nobody calls me that, which is okay because I really like insects. Most people don't, but—" She stopped. "You *are* the new girl, aren't you?" she asked, squinting at Meg anxiously. "The one Mr. Crockett sent me to get? Because if you're not, I'm going to feel pretty stupid and—"

"Oh, I am," Meg interrupted. She had a feeling you had to interrupt with Cricket. "I just moved here from Los Angeles. My name's Meg Kelly."

"Meg. I like that," said Cricket, as if she really did. "It reminds me of apple pie. You know, cinnamon, brown sugar, nutmeg. What a great dress!" she exclaimed as Meg got to her feet. "Kids in Redwood Grove wear such dull clothes. Jeans and sweaters. Sweaters and jeans. I like stuff that's more interesting."

That was easy to see! Still working on the connection between herself and apple pie, Meg took in Cricket's outfit. Besides an oversized green-and-white-striped shirt with a crazy array of buttons sewn down the front, she was wearing black leggings, yellow leg warmers, and pink high-tops with glittering silver laces. Meg had a feeling she hadn't gotten that outfit at Baylor's! It looked more like something she'd put together herself after scrounging around a Goodwill store and raiding her mother's button box. But it definitely had style. Even more than red boots and a suede jacket.

"You'd better take Meg back to class," Ms. Uchida warned. "You don't want Mr. Crockett sending out a search party."

"Oh. Right!" Cricket exclaimed, as if for a moment she'd forgotten why she'd been sent to the office. "Come on. Don't forget your lunch."

"My lunch?" Meg's spirits, which had been rising, took a nosedive. "But I didn't bring any lunch," she said, hurrying after Cricket into the hall. "Isn't there a cafeteria?"

"There is, but the food's barfo," Cricket replied, making a gagging sound in her throat. "Only little kids and kids who don't know any better eat there. But don't worry. You can eat lunch with me. My mom runs a catering business and I've always got tons of yummy stuff. Quiche and dolmas—that's stuffed grape leaves— sometimes chocolate truffles or lemon curd tarts . . ."

Her words flowed over Meg like warm chocolate syrup. Maybe Redwood Grove Elementary wouldn't be so bad, Meg thought cautiously. At least not at lunch!

The girls headed around a corner and down a hall lined with drawings of dinosaurs. "You're going to like Mr. Crockett," Cricket went on. "He's going to let us read real books instead of textbooks to learn about history and stuff, and later in the year we're going on a field trip to the Marine Mammal Center, and he's got all kinds of animals in the room. Snakes and iguanas and gerbils. I absolutely adore animals. I'm going to be a veterinarian or maybe a zoo keeper when I grow up. How about you?"

"Me?" Cricket's question caught Meg by surprise. Not that she didn't have an answer. She wanted to be a writer or maybe a private eye. But she didn't tell people that. It was a secret. Except, of course, from Jenny. "Oh, I don't know," she replied. "Maybe I'll be a . . . a teacher," she said, reaching for the first job she could think of.

"Well, that might be fun," said Cricket, though she sounded as if she didn't really believe it. "My dad's a teacher at the high school." She stopped in front of a blue door with a big 5A painted on it. "Of course, what he really wants to be is a writer. He's always . . . Oh—" She broke off in the middle of a sentence and pressed her hand against her nose. *"Ahchoo!"* she sneezed. "Hay fever," she explained. "It's awful this time of year and I never remember to bring Kleenex."

"Wait, I've got some," Meg said, reaching into her pocket for one of the Kleenex her mother had made sure she was carrying. As she did, Jenny's teddy bear tumbled out onto the floor. Meg made a dive for it, but Cricket beat her to it.

"A teddy bear! Oh, I love these little guys!" she exclaimed, scooping it up. "Just look at those big eyes and that silly smile. He's so dopey-looking!"

"No, he's not!" The words were out of Meg's mouth before she could stop them. She snatched the bear out of Cricket's hands.

"Gosh, I'm sorry," Cricket said, looking confused. "I didn't mean . . . Oh, I always put my foot in it." Her eyes were suddenly shiny.

Now I've done it, Meg thought. Talk about getting off on the wrong foot! She slipped the teddy bear back into her pocket and struggled to calm down. "It's all right. I don't know what came over me," she said quickly. "It's just that my best friend in Los Angeles, Jenny Snyder, gave it to me before I left and—" She stopped. Cricket had suddenly drawn in her breath. She looked at Meg as if she'd just seen a ghost.

"Jenny," she murmured. "You have a best friend named Jenny. I don't believe it! This is kismet, Meg Kelly. Kismet!"

C h a p t e r

What was she talking about? "Kismet?" Meg repeated. She wondered if the inside of Cricket's head was as scrambled as her outfit.

"Yes!" Cricket said excitedly. "Didn't you ever see that old movie on TV? It's about—"

But before she could begin to outline the plot of an old movie, the blue door to Room 5A opened and a man who looked a lot like Santa Claus—though with a much shorter beard—peered out.

"Mr. Crockett!" Cricket said. "This is Meg Kelly. She's from Los Angeles and she has a best friend named Jenny and—"

"Yes, Cricket," the teacher interrupted. Everyone seemed to realize that you had to interrupt with Cricket! "Thank you for escorting her from the office. Now if you'll just take your seat . . ." He stood aside so the girls could enter the room.

Cricket started to protest, but the look on Mr. Crockett's face—kind but firm—stopped her. "Lunchtime," she whispered quickly in Meg's ear as they went through the doorway. "I'll tell you then." She hurried to her desk at the far side of the room.

Meg hardly noticed she was gone. How could she when twenty-four pairs of eyes suddenly turned in her direction? She could feel them taking in her long blond hair and freckled nose, sizing up the flowered print dress and crocheted vest. But all that was nothing compared to what her own eyes were taking in!

"I see you've noticed our whale," said Mr. Crockett with a smile.

Noticed was an understatement! You didn't just notice a gigantic black-and-white whale hanging from the ceiling of a classroom. You stared, probably with your mouth hanging open, which was exactly what Meg was doing right now. Why hadn't Cricket told her about *this?*

"It's an orca," Mr. Crockett explained proudly. "A killer whale. Last year's fifth grade class made it out of papier mâché. This year we'll be working on a dolphin. I hope you like marine mammals, because we'll be learning a lot about them. Now let me see," he murmured. Putting a hand on Meg's shoulder, he guided her toward the front of the room, past a cage of iguanas and a terrarium holding what looked like a giant toad. "Where shall I put you? I try to keep things alphabetical at the beginning of the year. Makes it easier to learn

24

people's names. So that's *K* for Kelly, *L* for Logan. That's it. I'll put you right here beside Brittany Logan. Mark, could you pull over that extra desk?"

A good-looking boy with curly dark hair sprang to his feet. "Way to go, Mark," hooted a boy in a Batman sweatshirt as Mark flexed his muscles and grabbed the desk. A couple of girls giggled. Meg might have, too, except that she wasn't looking at Mark any longer. She was staring at the girl she was to sit beside. Brittany Logan—the girl in the limousine!

She'd taken off her suede jacket and draped it over the back of her chair, but it was her all right. Her long, tawny blond hair was sleek and shiny, framing her oval face. The creamy white blouse she'd been wearing under the jacket looked as if it might be made of silk. Still dazed by the spectacle of the whale hanging over her head—a sight only slightly more amazing than Brittany Logan—Meg sank down at the desk Mark had pushed into place.

"Fine," said Mr. Crockett. "Thank you, Mark. Now Brittany, if you'll share your book with Meg until I can get her one of her own, we'll start today's lesson. We do math first, while our brains are still working," he explained. "Now, who can tell me what a fraction is?"

Hands shot up.

Brittany Logan opened her math book and placed it so that it was half on her desk, half on Meg's.

"Thanks," Meg whispered, recovering her voice. From up close she could see that the lashes shading

Brittany's blue-gray eyes were incredibly long.

"Oh . . . yes . . . certainly," Brittany replied. She sounded startled, as if she wasn't used to being spoken to. The way she said the words sounded strange, too.

Meg looked at her curiously. Suddenly she remembered what she'd said in the office earlier, after apologizing to Ms. Uchida. *Mercy.* That was it, wasn't it? But what a peculiar thing to say. Why ask for mercy? It wasn't as if Ms. Uchida was going to send her to prison for being late! Then there was the nervousness and the quick little bow. . . .

Meg felt a familiar tingling sensation at the back of her neck. Her mother was always saying she saw mysteries where there weren't any, and maybe she was right. But Meg couldn't help it. Even though she was new, even though she was nervous and worried herself, an invisible detective hat slipped, unbidden, into place on her head. She was Meg Kelly, private eye. Meg Kelly, superspy!

She leaned across the desk toward Brittany. "I saw you in the office this morning," she whispered, as Mr. Crockett turned to write some numbers on the chalkboard.

Brittany looked startled. "You . . . you did?" she said.

"Yes. You said you were late because you missed the bus," Meg replied. "And you asked Ms. Uchida for—" She was about to go on, trying to find out what that plea for mercy had been about, but Brittany didn't give her a chance.

"Did you see the car?" she interrupted, a note of panic in her voice.

"The car?" Meg hesitated. She looked at Brittany. She knew that she wanted her to say no. She could see it in her eyes, hear it in her voice. Unfortunately Meg wasn't very good at lying. "Well . . . yes," she admitted. "I couldn't help it. It must be neat to have a limousine and a chauffeur."

"No, it's not," Brittany hissed. She glanced nervously at the boy sitting on the other side of her. "And if you dare tell anyone . . ."

"Girls!" Mr. Crockett frowned in their direction.

Brittany lowered her eyes immediately. But Meg could see that she was angry. Her jaw was clenched and a spot of red had appeared on each cheek.

From across the room, Cricket caught Meg's eye. She pointed at Brittany, under cover of her desk, and made a thumbs down sign. Then, as Mr. Crockett turned back to the chalkboard, she smiled and mouthed the word *lunchtime.*

Well, at least *she* hasn't given up on me, Meg thought as Brittany turned a chilly shoulder in her direction. She slipped her hand into the pocket where her teddy bear was hidden, suddenly feeling like the new girl again. How stupid it had been to practically snap Cricket's head off for saying the bear looked dopey.

She rubbed the bear's tummy with her thumb and

tried to think of Jenny. But instead she thought of Cricket. She remembered the excited look on her face and the word she had spoken. *Kismet.* That was what she'd said. But what in the world had she meant?

It took forever for lunchtime to come, and when the bell finally rang, Meg still wasn't free. Mr. Crockett had her stay for a few minutes so she could tell him where she was in math (behind) and in spelling (ahead). "I hope you like to read," he said, "because we do lots of independent reading in here. You'll catch up in math quickly. As for spelling, maybe you can help your neighbor Brittany Logan." He frowned slightly as if something about Brittany troubled him. "She's an interesting girl," he said. "New this year, just like you. I think she could use some extra help with spelling and vocabulary."

She could use some help with manners, too, Meg thought, though she didn't say it. But at least now she had a clue. If Brittany was new, maybe she was just nervous. Meg could certainly identify with that!

Mr. Crockett talked for awhile about how he wanted-ed everyone in 5A to feel like they were part of one big family. By the time he finally let Meg go, her stomach was rumbling and she was glad to find Cricket, lunch box in hand, waiting outside the classroom. A sturdy, round-faced girl was with her.

"Whew! I thought you'd never get out of there!" Cricket exclaimed. "This is Amy Chan."

"Hi," said Amy.

Meg recognized her as the girl who'd been sitting in front of Cricket in class. She wore blue sweatpants and a sweatshirt with *Redwood Grove Junior Soccer League* printed across the front. No creamy silk blouse and suede jacket for her! Amy's shiny black hair was caught up in two ponytails tied with red yarn.

"We thought you'd been eaten by the killer whale," she said, grinning at Meg.

"That whale—why didn't you tell me?" exclaimed Meg, forgetting about Brittany Logan and her fancy clothes. "I practically fainted when I saw it."

"I guess I forgot," Cricket admitted sheepishly. "You get kind of used to it hanging up there. It's really something, isn't it?" she said, as the girls headed out to the school yard. "I remember when the fifth grade was making it last year. Jenny and I would—"

"What?" Meg stopped in her tracks. She wasn't sure that she'd heard right. "Did you say Jenny?"

"Yes!" Cricket exclaimed. "That's what I was about to tell you in the hall this morning. That's what I meant by kismet!"

Amy rolled her eyes.

"Now don't be like that," Cricket said. "I know you don't believe in these things, Amy, but there's *got* to be something to it. Come on. Let's get ourselves a bench. Then I'll tell Meg and we'll let *her* decide."

Confused, Meg followed Cricket and Amy to one of the benches at the edge of the school yard where kids who had brought their lunches were eating. The yard was bordered by pine trees and the air was almost as crisp and clear as it had been earlier that morning. A couple of squirrels with big bushy tails—far bushier than the squirrels in Los Angeles had—were chasing each other up and down the branches, chattering and scolding as they went. But Meg wasn't interested in squirrels. Not now.

"Tell," she demanded, as they sat down on a bench.

Cricket didn't need to be asked twice. "All right," she said eagerly. "Here goes. That word I used—*kismet*—means fate, destiny. Something that's meant to happen."

"It's also the name of one of her favorite movies," Amy put in. "It's about a prince and a princess in India or somewhere who are nutty about each other but can't manage to get together. It's pretty sappy."

"It is not," objected Cricket. "It's beautiful. Romantic. And there's that wonderful song, remember? It goes like—"

"But what about Jenny?" Meg interrupted before Cricket could start singing. "What's an old movie got to do with her?"

"Not her—them!" Cricket exclaimed. "Don't you see?" she went on impatiently when Meg's face looked blank. "There are *two* Jennys. Your Jenny in Los Angeles—the one who gave you the teddy bear—and my Jenny—I mean, our Jenny . . ." She glanced quickly at Amy.

"No, that's okay," Amy assured her. "She was your friend more than mine. I moved here from San Francisco at the beginning of last year," she explained quickly to Meg. "But Cricket and Jenny were friends all their lives. Jenny moved to Alaska at the end of last year. But before that, she and Cricket lived right across the street from each other."

"Across the street? But that's exactly how it was with Jenny and me," Meg said in amazement, finally catching on to what Cricket was talking about. "We were at each other's houses all the time—playing games, doing homework, having sleepovers . . ."

"You see what I mean?" Cricket nodded knowingly, and even Amy looked impressed. "Kismet! We were meant to meet. Why else would Mr. Crockett have picked me instead of someone else to get you from the office?"

Meg didn't know. It could have been chance. But kismet sounded a lot more exciting!

"Well, I have to admit it is pretty remarkable," said Amy. "But I don't think we should encourage her, Meg," she added. "If we do she'll whip out her crystal ball or start reading our palms. Then we'll never get any lunch!"

Meg had nearly forgotten about eating, but the moment Cricket and Amy opened their lunch boxes, she remembered. "Are you sure you have enough?" she asked, suddenly feeling like an outsider again. "I've got my lunch money. I could eat in the cafeteria."

"And poison yourself? Are you kidding?" Cricket showed Meg her lunch box. "Look at all this. Mom catered a party at the garden club yesterday," she explained as she placed containers of shrimp and pasta salad, miniature cheese tarts, grilled chicken wings, and marinated mushrooms on the bench between them.

Amy set her own peanut butter and jelly sandwich aside and picked up a tart. "Don't be shy," she urged Meg between bites. "She's always got tons of stuff. We have to help her or she'll get fat as a blimp."

That was all the encouragement Meg needed. Still overwhelmed by all the stuff about the two Jennys, she picked up a chicken wing and bit into it. It was delicious!

For a while, all the girls did was eat. It wasn't until they'd polished off a pile of crisp, chocolate-covered cookies that Cricket called Florentines that Meg, feeling like she'd been going to Redwood Grove Elementary for years, suddenly remembered her desk mate.

She glanced quickly around the school yard. It was noisy and full of kids playing tetherball and tag, but she didn't see anyone with tawny hair and a suede jacket among them.

"I'm curious. What do you know about the girl sitting next to me in class?" she asked, the invisible detective hat slipping back on her head. "Brittany Logan."

"Her!" Amy snorted. "You mean Little Miss Nose-in-the-Air?"

Cricket shook her head. "I can't figure her out," she said, dumping the remains of their lunch in the trash. "She's new this year. I don't know where she came from, but when school started last week I tried to be nice. You know, just making conversation about movies and TV shows and stuff. But she wasn't very friendly. In fact, she looked like she didn't know what I was talking about."

"That's how she acted when I asked if she wanted to join the soccer team," said Amy. "And she doesn't ever come out here to play tetherball or anything. She must eat in the cafeteria and spend the rest of lunch hour in the library."

"I thought she looked like she was going to strangle you in class," said Cricket. "What did you say to her?"

"Not much really," Meg replied. "Just that I'd seen her while I was waiting in the office and . . ." She was about to go on, telling Cricket and Amy about the limousine and the chauffeur, but something stopped her. Brittany didn't want anyone to know about the limousine. That was clear. Even though she wasn't a friend, it didn't seem right to betray her. "I guess she's just nervous about being new," she finished quickly.

"But you're new and you don't act like that," Amy objected. "I say she's a snob! What do you say, Cricket?"

"Well, I don't know. There could be more to it than that," Cricket said.

"Oh, you always think there's more to things," grumbled Amy. "I know!" Her face suddenly lit up. "Let's find out. Let's spy on her!"

Meg hesitated. It sounded sort of sneaky. She wouldn't want anyone to spy on her just because she was new. But it also sounded like fun.

"Come on," Amy urged. "We'll see what we can find out this week. Then we'll compare notes. We'll have a sleepover at my house Friday night. Can you come?" she asked Meg.

"To a sleepover?" Meg repeated. Just this morning she'd been thinking that she'd never hear that word again. "A sleepover of spies?" She looked at Cricket to see what she thought.

"Why not?" agreed Cricket after a moment. "Brittany doesn't have to know about it. It can't do any harm."

Amy grinned. "This is going to be fun," she said, as Meg agreed. "We'll be solving a mystery, and it's already got a great title—'Who Is Brittany Logan?' "

Chapter

Unfortunately, Meg didn't have much time for spying after lunch. She had to spend the entire afternoon in a little room near the principal's office taking tests to find out how smart (or maybe how dumb!) she was. By the time she got back to Room 5A, the school day was nearly over and Mr. Crockett was making announcements.

"Finally, I have a new project to tell you about before you go home today," he was saying, as Meg slipped into her seat.

Brittany Logan glanced nervously in her direction, then looked away. Meg felt her cheeks get hot. A lot of good I am, she thought. I can't tell a lie and I feel like I have SPY written in big red letters across my forehead!

"As you've all heard me say," Mr. Crockett continued, "I want everyone in Room 5A to feel like they're part of one big family. To help things along, we're going to make a family bulletin board. I want each of you to bring in a picture of yourself as a baby. I'll put up the pictures and we'll see if we can guess who they are."

Oh no, Meg thought. All of their stuff, except for a few suitcases full of clothes, was in storage, waiting for her mother to find a house or apartment to rent. She knew they had photo albums—lots of them, full of pictures of her and Kevin as babies—but how would she ever be able to get to them?

She started to raise her hand to ask when they had to bring the pictures in, but a muffled sound—a sort of whispered groan—stopped her. She turned to see Brittany, her face almost as pale as her blouse, her fingers pressed against her lips.

"Are you all right?" she whispered quickly, forgetting about the baby pictures.

Brittany nodded. But she didn't look all right. She looked like Meg had felt when she'd come down with stomach flu last year. It had hit her right in the middle of class and she'd barely made it to the girls' room in time. Without thinking, she reached out to touch Brittany's arm.

Brittany drew back. Then, as the dismissal bell rang, she leaped from her seat and rushed down the aisle and out the door almost before Mr. Crockett could say, "Class dismissed."

Meg didn't know what to do. "Brittany, wait," she

called, as the class broke into noisy chatter and began streaming from the room. "Your jacket!" She plucked Brittany's suede jacket from where she'd left it on the back of her chair.

Cricket and Amy hurried across the room. "What's up?" Cricket said.

"What did you do?" asked Amy. "Tell her that jacket was made of dog skin?"

"I don't know," Meg replied, mystified. "She just suddenly gasped and looked sort of sick. I was afraid she was going to throw up."

"Let's check the girls' room," Cricket said, heading for the door. "Maybe she has some kind of deadly disease."

"Yeah, terminal snobbism!" said Amy. She was trying to be funny, but Meg could see she was concerned. Maybe Cricket was right. A deadly disease—maybe that was what was wrong with Brittany Logan!

They checked the girls' room at the end of the hall, and then another one near the office. But both were empty. By the time they made their way back through the crowded hall and out the front entrance, where kids were milling around laughing and shouting, Brittany was nowhere in sight. A school bus was pulling away from the curb. Meg didn't see any sign of a limousine.

"I guess she's gone," said Cricket. "What are you going to do with her jacket?"

"I suppose I'd better leave it in the office," Meg said, reluctant to part with the creamy-soft suede. "But wait," she said as she saw her mother among the crowd of parents and baby sitters on the sidewalk. "First I want you to meet my mom."

"It looks like she's already met mine," said Amy as the girls dashed down the steps and across the sidewalk. Mrs. Kelly was talking to a woman dressed in sweatpants and a sweatshirt like Amy.

"Meg!" she said as the girls joined them. "How'd it go?" Meg could see she was relieved that Meg wasn't alone. "Mrs. Chan's been recruiting me for the aerobics class she teaches," she went on. "I could certainly use it!"

"Well, drop by the studio anytime and pick up a schedule," said Amy's mother. Her sweatshirt had *Workout Workshop* printed across the front. "We'd love to have you. Now we have to run," she added, speaking to Amy. "You've got soccer practice and then we've got to get ready to go to your aunt's wedding in Sacramento tomorrow."

"Sacramento? Oh, no, I forgot! I won't be in school tomorrow," Amy said, turning to Cricket and Meg. Meg knew she was thinking of Brittany Logan, *not* of spelling and math!

"Well, I'm glad to hear you're so disappointed about missing school," laughed Mrs. Chan. "That's a good sign. Your brothers are jumping for joy. Now come on. You know how the coach hates it when you're late."

It wasn't until Mrs. Chan and Amy—with a whispered reminder about keeping an eye out for clues—

had jogged off down the block that Meg remembered she hadn't made any introductions. "Mom, I want you to meet Cricket Connors," she said. "She had a best friend named Jenny who moved away, and her mom has a catering business and—"

"Pleased to meet you," Cricket said, interrupting Meg and smiling quickly at Mrs. Kelly. Then she turned back to Meg. "Listen, why don't you come to my house tomorrow after school," she said. "Amy won't be here, but we can still talk about . . ." She let her voice trail off, but Meg knew who she meant. "Would that be all right?" Cricket asked Meg's mother. "It's not far from school. We can walk."

For a second, Mrs. Kelly seemed not to hear. She was looking at Cricket, a peculiar expression on her face.

"Mom," Meg prompted. "Can I go?"

"Oh. Oh, yes, of course."

"Great!" said Cricket, not seeming to notice anything strange. "See you tomorrow then. I'll show you my crystal ball," she added, and dashed off down the block.

Meg turned to her mother. "Mom, what's the matter with you?" she said, annoyed. "I introduce you to a new friend and you stare at her like she has two heads!"

"Oh dear, I'm sorry," Mrs. Kelly murmured. "But I just had the strangest feeling. Do you know that saying, 'A ghost walked over my grave'?"

"Mom, what are you talking about? Cricket's not a ghost!" said Meg.

"No, of course not," her mother agreed. "It's just an expression. But I do have a feeling I've seen that girl before." She shook her head. "No . . . it's more than that. I feel that I know her. But how could I?"

"Maybe it's kismet," said Meg with a laugh. Quickly she explained about Cricket and the two Jennys and kismet.

Mrs. Kelly laughed, too. "Well, I'm not sure I believe in *that*!" she said. She put her arm around Meg's shoulder and they headed for the car. "I'm sorry for acting so weird, and I'm really glad that you've made friends. Cricket and Amy both seem nice." She opened the car door. As she did, she noticed Brittany's jacket draped over Meg's arm. "Where in the world did you get that?" she asked.

Meg had forgotten she was holding the jacket. She glanced toward the school, but it seemed too late now to take it to the office. "The girl who sits next to me forgot it," she explained. "She . . . she left in a hurry. I'll return it to her tomorrow."

"Well, be sure you remember," said Mrs. Kelly, taking the jacket from Meg and examining it. "This is a very expensive garment. I'm surprised it belongs to a child." She glanced at the label sewn inside the neck. "Well, look at that!" she exclaimed. "It's an Adrienne Logan!"

"Adrienne *Logan*," Meg repeated. She leaned over

to read the label sewn inside the jacket. *An Adrienne Logan Design, Paris—New York* said the words embroidered in elegant gold thread on a black satin rectangle.

"She's a well-known fashion designer," said Mrs. Kelly as she smoothed the jacket, folded it carefully, and placed it on the back seat of the car. "Don't expect to find anything this fancy at Baylor's. Not that I could afford to buy it if you did," she added with a smile. "Now let's go. We may not be in the Adrienne Logan league, but it's shop until we drop time for us, Meg!"

Meg climbed into the car and buckled her seat belt, hardly noticing what she was doing. That label was a clue if ever there was one! Of course, Logan was a fairly common name. They weren't necessarily related. But suppose Adrienne Logan *was* Brittany's mother. That would explain the limousine and chauffeur. Famous designers who created expensive clothes probably made plenty of money.

She felt like racing to a phone to call Cricket and Amy. Then she remembered that she didn't have their phone numbers. She wouldn't be able to tell anyone anything until tomorrow!

"Meg, are you still here?" Mrs. Kelly said, pulling into a parking spot in front of Baylor's Children's Apparel. "You look like you're on another planet."

"I'm okay, Mom," said Meg quickly, struggling to put Brittany out of her mind. Luckily, Baylor's was having a sale, just as Ms. Uchida had said. As soon as

Meg walked through the door and saw the tables piled high with clothes marked 50 percent off, her detective hat went off and her fashion hat went on.

"Now remember, it gets colder up here than in Los Angeles," Mrs. Kelly said. "You'll need plenty of sweaters and a warm jacket."

They searched through the tables and racks of clothes, and though they didn't quite shop until they dropped, Meg did manage to get more new school clothes than she ever had before. Remembering what most of the girls (except for Cricket and Brittany Logan!) were wearing, she decided she'd rather fit in than make a fashion statement. She stuck mostly to sweaters and jeans, though she did get one outfit she was sure Cricket would approve of—a tie-dyed shirt and a pair of purple overalls splashed with gold sunbursts—both of them 75 percent off!

When they were done at Baylor's, they went next door to a women's dress shop called Savvy Lady. "I'm not sure how people will dress at my new job," Mrs. Kelly said, as she worked her way through a rack of suits and blouses. "I don't want to look completely out of place on my very first day."

Meg was surprised. Somehow she hadn't thought mothers worried about stuff like that. "Don't worry. You'll look fine, Mom," she said. "You always do."

Mrs. Kelly laughed. "It seems to me I said those very same words to you this morning. I guess nothing changes, Meg. Except Redwood Grove! I can't believe all the expensive shops this town has now. And those fancy houses being built in the hills are practically mansions. I wonder if any of my old hangouts are left."

It turned out that not many were. After Meg and her mother finished shopping, they left the clothes in the car and took a sentimental journey through town. The five-and-ten cent store, where Mrs. Kelly said you'd actually been able to buy things for a nickel, was gone. The old Redwood Grove Bakery, whose jelly doughnuts she remembered with fondness, had been replaced by a fancy pastry shop called Sweet Temptations. And the hardware store was now a bed-and-bath shop full of lacy linens and icky-sweet soaps.

"I know one place that hasn't changed," said Mrs. Kelly. "My favorite—Elmer's Ice Cream Emporium. Shall we give it a try?"

Meg could hardly say no to ice cream!

"No need to tell Kevin about this," her mother whispered conspiratorially as they slipped into a booth at the back of the old-fashioned ice cream shop. "Grandma's probably filling him up with chocolate chip cookies right now anyway, and it's nice to have some time to ourselves. I think I'll have a root beer float. That's what Karen Parker and I always ordered."

"Karen Parker?" Meg hadn't heard that name before.

"Yes. She was my best friend when I was growing up here in Redwood Grove," Mrs. Kelly replied. "I haven't thought of her in years, but back then we did everything together. Went on hikes, had sleepovers at each other's houses, hung out here at Elmer's. Why, we even had a—"

"What happened to her?" Meg interrupted, suddenly interested. If Karen had been her mother's best friend then and she wasn't now, surely something terrible must have happened.

"Oh, she moved," Mrs. Kelly said. "Her father got a new job. In Oregon, as I remember. And then . . . well, we just sort of lost touch." She sighed. "That's what happens when people move away from each other. You promise to write and then—" She stopped. "Oh, but that won't happen with you and Jenny," she said quickly. "You'll always be friends. I just know it."

She sounded positive, but Meg knew she was just trying to make her feel better. She drained the strawberry soda she'd ordered and thought about the ad for the airplane ticket that was tucked away in her stationery box. Now that she'd met Cricket and Amy, the idea of flying to Los Angeles and moving in with Jenny seemed sort of silly. Then she thought of something. Jenny could come here! Not to live, of course, but to visit. She'd like Amy and Cricket and they would like her. The four of them could do things together. Of course, there was still the problem of money. . . .

"Meg?" Her mother's voice broke into her thoughts. "You're on another planet again and we'd better get home." She paid for the sodas. "Kevin's dying to tell you about those rabbits at his nursery school. And, oh, I almost forgot. The computer my company's giving me arrived today. You can help me set it up."

Meg had forgotten about the computer, too. It was hard to imagine one in her grandparents' big old house in the redwoods. The place seemed so old-fashioned. It had a big stone fireplace in the living room, a huge claw-footed tub in the bathroom, and a preserve-filled pantry off the kitchen. A wide porch with a swing on it went all the way around the house from front to back.

The only thing missing, Meg thought, as her mother brought the car to a halt in the driveway, was a big treasure-filled attic. But maybe that would make the house too perfect! She jumped out of the car and dashed up the steps to the porch. There was a door knocker in the shape of a dolphin that Meg loved to use, but today she didn't get a chance. Before she could reach the front door, Kevin came charging out.

"Mom, Grandma can work the computer!" he said. "She can draw pictures, Meg. She's going to teach me. Come and see." He grabbed his sister by the hand and dragged her into the house.

"Janet, is that you?" Grandma called from the study.

Meg's mother dropped the packages she was carrying on the hall table. "Mother, you shouldn't have—" she began, then stopped herself.

"Oh, it's all right," said Grandma, poking her head out of the study. "I've been taking a class in computers at the Senior Center. I think they're fascinating. Come see, Meg."

For a moment Meg was torn. She loved her grandmother. She loved her silvery gray hair and her wrinkly skin and the way she was interested in so many things. But she knew that sometimes Grandma got on her mother's nerves. This time, though, Mrs. Kelly just smiled and shook her head, the way she did when Kevin tracked mud in the house. "Go on, Meg," she said. "Grandma seems to know what she's doing. I'll be along soon."

Meg's grandmother really did have the computer working. She was showing Kevin how to use a drawing program. "Watch this," he said proudly, taking the mouse in his hand and moving it around on the desk. A scribbly drawing appeared on the screen. "It's a rabbit, just like they got . . . I mean, just like they have . . . in my school."

Meg tried out a game produced by the company her mother was going to work for. It was okay, but she got bored trying to rescue the princess. Why don't these games ever have you rescue a prince? she thought.

She tried a writing program, and then her mother hooked up the printer. They printed out Kevin's rabbit and a poem Meg wrote for her grandmother. It went: Roses are red, Violets are blue, Better cook dinner, Before I eat you!

Grandma laughed when she read it. "I would," she said, "except that your grandfather insisted on trying out a new recipe tonight. He's at Harvey's Health Foods right now, picking up the ingredients."

"Oh, no," Meg groaned. "Can't we just send out for pizza?"

She was only half-kidding. When Grandpa had retired, he'd taken up cooking. Not ordinary cooking—healthy cooking. Not that there was anything wrong with that. Cricket's mother could probably make health food delicious. Unfortunately, Grandpa hadn't stumbled on the secret yet.

Tonight, he whipped up a casserole of carrots, Brussels sprouts, brown rice, and tofu—cubes of tasteless white stuff made of soybeans—that must have been just bursting with vitamins but that tasted like wet dog biscuits. A dash of ketchup would have been an improvement, but Meg's grandfather didn't see it that way. At the end of the meal, he stretched out his lean frame—kept trim by hours of jogging and long bird-watching trips—and patted his stomach contentedly. "Notice how your taste buds become attuned to the natural flavors of the food," he said. "Now that's how you ought to feed these children, Janet!"

Meg's mother gave her a warning glance, but she didn't need to worry. Meg wasn't about to mention their visit to Elmer's. Grandma scooped up Kevin before he had a chance to say anything about chocolate chip cookies and whisked him, protesting loudly, off to his bath.

"Meg, why don't you tell your grandfather about school," said Mrs. Kelly quickly.

Meg knew she was trying to change the subject, but she didn't mind. There was so much to tell. She began with the whale hanging from the ceiling and moved on to the dolphin they were going to build. Then she remembered the family bulletin board.

"Mom, I need a baby picture," she said, explaining quickly about Mr. Crockett's assignment. "Are all our photos packed away?"

"Oh dear, I'm afraid they are," replied her mother. "We won't be able to get into any of those boxes until we get the stuff out of storage. It could take weeks, maybe longer."

"But Mom, I can't be the only one in class without a picture," Meg protested. "I don't want people to think I'm an orphan."

"Now, don't go feeling sorry for yourself," said Grandpa. "I'm sure we've got lots of pictures right here. Why, I seem to remember carrying a big box of old photos up to the attic just before—"

"The attic?" Meg stared at her grandfather. She couldn't be hearing right. This house didn't have an attic.

"Now you've done it," her mother murmured, shaking her head at Grandpa as she began to clear the dishes from the table. "You'd better come clean."

"Come clean? You mean there really *is* an attic?" Meg exclaimed. She felt like the girl in that book who finds a secret garden hidden away behind a locked door. "But where is it?" she demanded. "How do you get into it? Why didn't anyone ever tell me about it before?"

Grandpa looked at Meg's mother, but she gave him no help. "Well, I guess the cat's out of the bag," he said. "I'd better tell you. It's not really an attic, though. It's more like a storage space. We never mentioned it because it's not a very safe place for little kids like Kevin to go. You see, you have to get up to it"—his eyes were twinkling mischievously now—"by way of a secret stairway."

"A secret stairway!" Naturally, Meg wanted to see the attic right then and there. But her grandfather, who was something of a trickster, was enjoying himself too much.

"Tomorrow," he promised. "I wouldn't want to spoil the fun you'll have imagining what's up there by showing you too soon."

"Oh, Dad, you're too much." Meg's mother laughed.

"I won't be able to sleep if I don't know," Meg threatened. But it was no use. She couldn't get another word out of either of them.

She was right about not sleeping. Lying in bed in the room that used to be her mother's, Meg stared out the window at the dark shapes of the redwood trees silhouetted by the moon. She tried closing her eyes, but they popped open again. She turned over on her stomach and buried her head under her pillow, but it was no use.

Finally, Meg sat up, switched on the light, and opened the night table drawer. She took out a pencil and her stationery box. Choosing a sheet of paper with a border of hearts that was lying just on top of the airplane ad, she began to write.

Dear Jenny,

I hardly know where to begin. So many things have happened. I met a girl named Cricket and another girl named Amy. We're trying to solve a mystery. And you'll never believe what I found out about this house . . .

C h a p t e r

4

A secret attic!" Cricket exclaimed. The morning bell was ringing and the girls were hurrying down the noisy, crowded halls of Redwood Grove Elementary School toward Room 5A. "Meg, that is *so* exciting. But didn't you look for it?" she asked.

"Of course I did," said Meg, remembering how she'd leaped out of bed the moment her alarm went off and begun searching the second floor of her grandparents' house, opening doors, peering into closets and rooms. She'd even run her hands over the walls to see if she could find a door cut into the paneling. But there was nothing. No hidden doorway, no secret staircase, no way at all to get into an attic.

Grandpa was no help because he'd left at dawn to go on a birdwatching trip with the Audubon Society. Grandma was no help, either. Her lips were sealed, she said—she'd promised Grandpa. As for Meg's mother, she was too busy rushing around dressing Kevin, putting on makeup, and trying to find a scarf to go with her Savvy Lady suit to pay much attention to Meg.

Maybe the attic isn't even there, Meg thought, feeling discouraged. She did discover two small round windows high up under the eaves of her grandparents' house that she hadn't noticed before. They might be false, though, purely for decoration. In fact, the whole thing might be false, some kind of elaborate joke that her grandfather had dreamed up.

"It's too bad Amy's not here," said Cricket now. "She's good at doing puzzles and figuring things out. But I'll bet the two of us could find it if we really searched."

That was exactly what Meg had been hoping she would say. "Then come over this afternoon and help me look," she urged. "My mother will be at work, Grandpa went birdwatching, and Grandma will probably be at the park with Kevin. We'll have the place to ourselves. If there's an attic up there, we should be able to find it."

Cricket didn't need any more convincing. "It's a deal!" she said, as they reached the classroom. "Only we'll have to go to my house first. My mom asked me to stop on the way home to pick up some vanilla beans from her friend who runs Sweet Temptations—that's a bakery. I'll have to ask permission to go to your house, too, but I'm sure my mom won't mind. She's dying to meet you. She said she knows just how you must feel about moving because she had to move, too, when she was a girl. She also said she's going to be trying out some new recipes this afternoon, so we're sure to get tastes. And . . ."

She hesitated. "And there's something else," she said, lowering her voice. She pulled Meg aside, out of the stream of kids entering the room. "When we get to my house, I want to show you something. It's not something I'd show to just anyone, but I feel like . . . well . . . like I've known you for a long, long time. Longer than Amy, longer than my friend Jenny, even. I know it doesn't make sense. I can't explain it, but . . . this thing I want to show you means a lot to me and it's really, really sad."

"Sad?" Meg looked at Cricket curiously. She didn't seem like someone who'd had a lot of sadness in her life. Meg had known her only one day, but she would have sworn Cricket was someone who was always cheerful and chirpy—just like her name. "Cricket, what is it?" she asked.

But Cricket wouldn't tell. "I don't want to talk about it now," she said quickly. "I can't. But you'll see." Then, as if to change the subject, she asked, "Where's Brittany Logan's jacket? Didn't you bring it back?"

"Oh, no!" Meg groaned. In her mind's eye, she saw the toffee-colored suede jacket lying on a chair in the hallway of her grandparents' house. "I forgot!" She'd also forgotten, in all the excitement about the attic, to tell Cricket about the label in the jacket. But there was no time now. The tardy bell was ringing and Mr. Crockett was herding stragglers, including Meg and Cricket, into the room.

Meg headed for her desk, hoping that Brittany wouldn't be too upset. She imagined her leaping to her feet, pointing an accusing finger, and yelling "Thief!" But nothing of the sort happened. Brittany wasn't there. She didn't come in after the tardy bell had stopped ringing. She didn't show up during math, or language arts, or at lunchtime. The entire day passed, and the seat beside Meg remained empty.

"I guess she really was sick," Meg said when school was finally over and the girls were heading for Sweet Temptations. She'd told Cricket at lunchtime about the label in the jacket, but somehow, without Amy and with the thought of the secret attic lying ahead of them, spying on Brittany didn't seem quite so exciting.

"Well, I hope she's all right," said Cricket. "She might not be the nicest person in the world, but it's no fun being sick—especially sick to your stomach. I do think it was pretty clever of you, though, to figure out her mother is a fashion designer."

"But I didn't figure that out," Meg objected. "Not exactly. We don't know for sure that her mother designed that jacket. Adrienne Logan could be her aunt or a cousin. Or they might not be related at all."

"Well, it's still a clue," Cricket insisted, opening the

door of the pastry shop. "And you were smart to think of a connection. That's what real detectives do—at least the ones I've seen on TV. Amy's going to be impressed," she added.

Meg couldn't help feeling flattered. But her pride was quickly overwhelmed by hunger as the delicious aroma of chocolate and freshly baked bread hit her nose. The sight of the pastry-filled display cases inside Sweet Temptations made her feel almost weak at the knees.

"Hi, Cricket," a woman behind the counter said with a smile. "Your mom said you'd come by. Have a taste of these while I get the vanilla beans." She handed the girls chocolate chip cookies still warm from the oven.

Meg bit into one hungrily. It was much better than her lunch—a tofu and bean sprout sandwich that her grandfather had thoughtfully packed and left for her before he'd gone on his birdwatching trip. She'd had a few bites of Cricket's goodies, of course, but it didn't seem right to keep freeloading.

"I'd rather have a mother in the food business than the fashion business any day," she said as they left the pastry shop with a sack full of vanilla beans and a couple of extra cookies in hand.

"Yeah, but you don't get rich baking brownies," Cricket said. "Famous fashion designers probably have yachts and drive around in—Hey, look at that!" She broke off in the middle of her sentence. A limousine had just pulled into a parking space down the block. The chauffeur got out and started to walk around to the back door, but before he could reach it, the door opened and—

Meg felt like she was watching a replay of a movie as Brittany Logan, wearing gray leggings and a long pink sweater, got out. This time she wasn't alone, though. She was followed by an elegant-looking woman dressed all in beige.

"Quick," Meg said, grabbing Cricket by the arm and dragging her into a nearby doorway. Brittany hadn't seen them, but there was no sense taking chances.

"I don't believe it," Cricket murmured, peeking out from the doorway as the woman in beige said something to the chauffeur and then hurried after Brittany, who was striding quickly down the block.

"I do," said Meg. "She didn't want me to tell anyone, but that's the way she got to school yesterday."

"In a limousine?" Cricket looked as if she still couldn't believe it. "What should we do? Follow them?"

Meg didn't have to think twice. She knew it was sneaky, but she had to find out. Was the woman in beige Brittany's mother? Was she Adrienne Logan of Paris and New York?

"Yes," she whispered to Cricket. "But be careful. Don't let her see us."

The girls stepped out of the doorway. Brittany was moving purposefully down the block, her mother—if that's who it was—at her heels. She passed a drugstore but didn't stop, so they weren't going to pick up medicine. Not that Brittany looked the least bit sick. Her cheeks weren't pale, as they had been yesterday. Nor were they red, as they would be if she had a fever.

When she approached the Redwood Grove Pet Shop, her pace slowed slightly. Was she going to get her mother to buy her one of the Siamese kittens frisking in the window? Meg wondered. But no. With no more than a brief glance at the blue-eyed kittens, she moved on quickly.

Meg and Cricket, keeping close to the buildings, followed Brittany past a bookstore, a jewelry shop, and a bank, until she came to a store with *Village Stationers* painted in gold on its plate-glass windows. Then she stopped.

Meg and Cricket stopped, too. Brittany turned. Had she seen them? No, she was saying something to the woman a step or two behind her. When the woman caught up, the two of them disappeared into the shop.

Meg let out her breath, which she hadn't realized she'd been holding. "Come on," she said, not bothering to whisper as she headed down the block. She reached the stationery store and ducked down. Motioning for Cricket to do the same, she crept past the plate-glass windows and into the shop. It was filled with all sorts of paper supplies—notebooks, stationery, calendars— plus shelves of music boxes, clocks, stuffed animals, and knickknacks.

Meg couldn't see Brittany anywhere. Could she have already left by the rear door? Then Cricket pointed toward the back of the store.

"Look. There they are," she whispered. She grabbed Meg by the arm and pulled her between two rows of greeting cards. Hardly daring to breathe, the girls crept past get-well wishes, wedding announcements, birthday greetings, and bar mitzvah congratulations. When they reached the end of the row, they peeked around a rack of postcards to see Brittany and the woman in beige examining a display of picture frames.

"I don't understand why you need a frame for your father's picture right now," the woman was saying. From up close, Meg could see how beautifully she was dressed. Her beige slacks and jacket fit to perfection. Her dark hair was drawn back in a sleek twist held in place by a tortoiseshell comb. "You stayed home sick today. You should be resting."

"I told you. I'm all right now, Mother," Brittany insisted.

Meg and Cricket exchanged a glance. So this *was* Brittany's mother!

"It must have been something I ate," Brittany went on, her cheeks coloring slightly, just the way Meg's did when she was telling a lie. "And I need the frame because I . . . because I'm decorating my room." She turned away from her mother quickly and peered at the frames.

Mrs. Logan sighed. "Well, all right," she said. "I want you to be happy with your room. I know how much things like that matter. How about this one?" She picked up a silver frame with a picture of a smiling young man in it. "This is very tasteful. Though I don't know why they always include these ridiculous photos," she added. "Except to give work to the models."

Brittany glanced at the frame, then shook her head. "No, not that one. I want something more like . . ." She reached for a small, plain plastic frame at the back of the shelf. "Like this," she said, holding it out.

Mrs. Logan made a face. "But Brittany, that's so . . . tacky," she said. "It's a sweet-looking baby," she added, glancing at the picture in the frame. "But plastic? Really, it won't do at all. *C'est trop . . .*"

All at once, Meg had no idea what they were saying. A whole torrent of words came tumbling out of Mrs. Logan's mouth. And Brittany was responding with the same kind of words. But Meg had no idea what they meant.

Cricket looked just as mystified. "They must be speaking some other language," she said, forgetting to keep her own voice down.

Brittany turned to look in their direction, but the girls ducked behind the bar mitzvah cards just in time.

"Well, all right, if this is the one you really want," Mrs. Logan said, returning to English. She took the frame and headed for the cash register at the front of the store. Brittany, a relieved look on her face, followed.

There was some more conversation that Meg couldn't understand. Then Mrs. Logan handed the saleswoman her charge card and signed the receipt. In a few minutes, she and Brittany were gone.

Meg and Cricket popped out from between the rows of greeting cards and rushed to the window. They were just in time to see Brittany climb into the limousine. She pulled the door shut and the car drove away.

"Well, isn't that something," the saleswoman murmured, looking over the girls' shoulders. "Friend of yours?"

"Sort of," Cricket replied. "Did you understand what they were saying?"

"Not when they spoke French," the saleswoman said with a laugh. "I took it for two years in high school, but all I can remember is *merci,* which means thank you."

"Thank you?" Meg echoed. *Merci?* So that's what Brittany had been saying in the office! She hadn't been pleading for mercy. She'd been thanking Ms. Uchida in French!

"Beautiful woman," the saleswoman commented, stepping back behind the counter. "Lovely name, too. Seems familiar somehow. Adrienne," she said, as Meg and Cricket exchanged an excited glance. "Adrienne Logan. You girls ever heard that name before?"

Chapter

Meg didn't know how they reached Cricket's house. After they left the stationery shop, they were talking so much that she barely noticed the streets they went down or the corners they turned—to say nothing of the stores, houses, and front yards they passed. What they were talking about, of course, was Brittany.

"Imagine being able to speak French like that," Meg said. She knew kids who could speak Spanish. She could even say a few words herself, but somehow that didn't seem so exotic. "I'll bet she moved here from France. Isn't Paris the capital? The label in her jacket said 'An Adrienne Logan Design, Paris—New York.' "

"But neither of them really sounded French. I mean, not when they were speaking English," Cricket said. "They didn't have accents. Maybe they live part of the time in Paris and part in New York. Brittany must have gone to a French school, though. Maybe that's why she doesn't play tetherball. Maybe they don't have games like that in France!"

"Probably a lot of things are different," said Meg, thinking about how different things were just between Los Angeles and Redwood Grove—and they were in the same state! "It must be hard, going back and forth between two languages," she added. "I'd always be afraid I was going to say the wrong thing."

They walked on in silence for a while then. Meg remembered how nervous Brittany had been in the office, and later when Meg had spoken to her in class. Meg also remembered how worried she had been that first morning when she didn't know if she was wearing the right thing or if she'd ever make friends. Suddenly she felt ashamed of herself. Brittany was new to the country, she was having trouble with the language, and all she and Cricket and Amy could do was label her a snob!

Cricket must have been thinking the same thing. "I guess it might even be hard being rich," she said, breaking the silence as they turned a corner onto a pleasant block of small houses with neat front yards. "Riding around in a limousine sounds like fun, but I can see how you might get tired of people staring at you. And then there are all those expensive clothes she wears. They might be the height of fashion somewhere, but they don't exactly help her fit in at Redwood Grove Elementary

School! In fact, I wonder why she's going to our school at all. You'd think someone like her would go to a fancy private school. There are plenty of them around here—probably even some where they speak French."

Meg hadn't lived in Redwood Grove long enough to know about that. But she did wonder about Brittany's behavior when she'd seemed to be sick. "She certainly looked like something was wrong yesterday," she said, "but I could swear she was lying about it today."

"If she was lying, though, why drag her mother downtown to buy a plastic picture frame?" said Cricket. "Everyone knows if you're going to stay home from school pretending to be sick, you've got to keep it up at least until dinnertime. She could have run into Mr. Crockett or the principal. Then she'd really have been in trouble!"

Cricket was right. And why had Brittany been so determined to have that tacky little plastic frame when her mother would have been more than happy to buy a beautiful silver one? It didn't make sense. It was like a puzzle with a piece missing. But before Meg could think any more about it, Cricket turned off the sidewalk and announced, "We're here!"

She led the way up a brick walk, bordered with parsley and chives, to a pretty blue house with white shutters and a bright yellow door. The moment she opened the door, a tantalizing aroma hit Meg's nose.

"Cricket?" a voice called. A second later a slim,

red-headed woman wearing a denim shirt and jeans, carrying a mixing bowl in one hand and a wooden spoon in the other, appeared. "Ah! You must be Meg," she said, smiling warmly. "I'm Cricket's mom."

She didn't need to tell Meg that! Even if they hadn't been in the Connors's house, even if they'd been in a crowd somewhere, Meg would have immediately matched her to Cricket. Except for the difference in their ages, the two looked so much alike they could almost have been twins. Meg wondered if *Mr.* Connors had the same red hair, blue eyes, and freckles. What she really wondered, though, was what was cooking.

"What is that?" she asked, forgetting her manners and sniffing the air. The rich, spicy smell also made her forget all about picture frames and limousines and French fashion designers. She remembered the dinner her grandfather had cooked last night. Meg had a feeling that whatever Cricket's mother was whipping up in the kitchen, it didn't include tofu and she hadn't shopped for the ingredients at Harvey's Health Foods. But she was wrong.

"I'm experimenting," Mrs. Connors said. "Come and be my taste tester." She led the way into a big, bright kitchen. French doors opened out onto a flower-filled backyard. Gleaming copper pots hung from a rack above the stove, and jars of spices, bowls of fruit, and baskets of vegetables were everywhere.

Mrs. Connors lifted the lid from a blue-enameled pot on the stove. The fragrant-smelling steam that escaped from it made Meg's mouth water. Mrs. Connors dipped in a spoon and held it out. "Careful, it's hot," she warned.

Meg took a taste. It was even better than it smelled. "What is this?" she asked, licking the spoon clean.

"Vegetable stew made with eggplant and tofu," Cricket's mother replied. "No salt, no fat, lots of natural flavor from herbs and spices, chock full of vitamins and protein. I'm trying to develop some good-tasting, healthy recipes for my business. Harvey at the health food store has been giving me tips. It's not bad, is it?"

"Not bad? It's terrific!" said Meg enthusiastically. "My grandfather shops at Harvey's, but nothing he cooks tastes this good. Maybe you could give him the recipe."

"I'd be glad to," said Mrs. Connors, looking pleased.

"She could use some ideas for lunches, too," Cricket said, handing her mother the vanilla beans they'd picked up at Sweet Temptations. "You should have seen the miserable sandwich she brought today. Dad and I are trying to convince Mom to write a cookbook," she added. "Mainly because we like to taste-test the recipes." She paused. Then, "Pete liked to taste them, too," she said, speaking quickly, as if she wanted to get the words out of her mouth fast before she could stop them.

Meg saw a look of concern come over Mrs. Connors's face. "Now, Cricket . . ." she began.

She remembered what Cricket had said that morning about wanting to show her something sad. Was this it? Something about this person named Pete?

"Don't worry, Mom. I'm not going to start blubbering," Cricket said. "I just want to show her."

"Show me?" repeated Meg, as Cricket grabbed her by the arm and pulled her out the French doors to the backyard. "Show me what?"

"A grave," Cricket replied, heading across the lawn with Meg in tow. "Pete's grave."

Meg caught her breath. Graves were for dead people. They belonged in cemeteries, not in people's backyards. She pulled back, but Cricket had her firmly in hand.

"He was only a few years older than me when he died," she rushed on. "He loved the backyard, so we buried him out here under his favorite tree. See." She came to a halt in front of a graceful willow at the corner of the yard and let go of Meg's arm. "There. That's what I wanted to show you."

Meg stared at the varnished wooden plaque. *Pete, Faithful Friend and Companion,* read the inscription. *Champion Frisbee Player.*

"I wish you'd known him," Cricket said, her voice suddenly husky. "He was wonderful. We buried him with his Frisbee because he loved it so much. That and his favorite chew stick. Dad wrapped him up in his old plaid blanket and—"

"A dog," Meg interrupted. "Pete was a dog."

"Well, of cou___" said Cricket. "You didn't think—Oh, no, you did, di____ ou?"

"No I didn't," M_____ _lied, crossing her fingers behind her back. She ___d see that Cricket wasn't fooled, but she was too e___ ⟲o tell Meg about Pete to argue.

"I couldn't talk about him at school this morning," she explained, "because sometimes I get all choked up. The day after he died, I had to stay home. I couldn't even get out of bed. He used to sleep in my room, and he'd wait by the window for me to come home from school. Mom and Dad had him before I was born, so he was always around. I guess I thought he always would be. Then this summer his . . . his heart just gave out."

Meg didn't know what to say. She'd never had a dog. But Jenny did—a floppy-eared cocker spaniel named Randy. It wasn't hard to imagine how upset she'd be if he died. "What kind of a dog was he?" she asked. She'd heard her mother say that it was helpful to get people to talk about their losses, even if you thought it might upset them. It seemed to work.

"A golden retriever," Cricket replied, looking relieved, as if she'd been afraid Meg might laugh at the way she felt about Pete, or say it didn't matter because he was only a dog. "He was beautiful. Kind of honey-colored with the silkiest fur."

"Have you . . ." Meg hesitated. She didn't want to hurt Cricket's feelings, but . . . "Have you thought about getting another one?" she asked. "I mean, I'm sure no one could take his place. But you could get a puppy. Maybe the same kind."

"Oh, Meg," Cricket said. "I was right about showing you this. I knew you'd understand. That's *exactly* what I want to do. There's a kennel near here that breeds golden retrievers. One of them is expecting a litter of puppies any day now. The trouble is they cost two hundred dollars and my parents can't afford to spend that much right now. But if I could come up with half—one hundred dollars—they might put up the other half. I've got some money saved, but nowhere near that amount. Only about ten dollars, actually. I don't know how I could ever get so much money."

Neither did Meg. She thought about Jenny and the $99 airfare from Los Angeles. "It's a lot for one person to earn," she said. "Especially someone our age. We're not even old enough to baby-sit."

Cricket sighed. "I know. I keep thinking of what I could sell," she said. "I've got a seashell collection in my room. Come on, I'll show you." She led the way back into the house. "I don't know if it's worth much, though. Then there's the petrified rock my grandfather gave me, and my Madame Alexander dolls. But I couldn't part with them, so . . ." She threw open the door to her room. "Ta-da," she said with a flourish.

Meg hadn't thought about how Cricket's room would look, but when she saw it, she wasn't surprised. It looked like Cricket. Original. Just like her clothes.

The headboard of the bed was upholstered with bright butterfly-printed fabric. The drawers of the dresser were painted all the colors of the rainbow, from purple at the bottom to red at the top. A kite with a dragon face and a long multi-colored tail was tacked to one wall. Posters of all kinds of animals—dogs, horses, gorillas, and dolphins—plus a few of Meg's favorite TV stars and music groups covered the others. Albums and boxes of photos were spread out on the floor. The seashell collection was arranged on a shelf above the dresser. Meg didn't think it was worth a hundred dollars.

Cricket picked up one of the photo albums. "You know, when I got these albums out last night, I was thinking about those puppies," she said. "I kept hoping that maybe I'd find a savings bond or a stock certificate tucked in with the baby pictures, but—"

"Baby pictures," Meg interrupted. She suddenly remembered Mr. Crockett and the family bulletin board and the pictures she'd asked her mother about last night. "The attic! In my grandparents' house. I forgot all about it!"

From the look on her face it was clear that Cricket had, too. But she made up for it, as they rushed to the kitchen to get her mother's permission to go. "Just imagine what's stored up there," she said. "Old clothes, dolls, jewelry, chests of gold doubloons. Maybe even a skeleton or two!"

Meg knew she was kidding about the skeleton, but

what Cricket said made her think. Maybe there *was* a treasure in the attic. Not a chest full of jewels or gold, but maybe a shoe box full of valuable old baseball cards or an album of priceless postage stamps. Maybe it wouldn't be so hard to get money for an airline ticket or a golden-colored puppy. Maybe it was waiting for them right now, at the top of her grandparents' house!

When they got to the kitchen, they found Cricket's mother up to her elbows in bread dough. "Just leave your grandparents' number on the pad by the telephone," she said. "Give me a call if you need me to pick you up later, Cricket. And help yourselves to some of those cookies I just took out of the oven. Only the broken ones, though. I'm saving the whole ones for the Film Society buffet."

Meg was glad to have a few cookies, broken or not, to munch on as they raced out the door and down the block. She had a feeling she was going to need plenty of energy!

"We've got to think logically," Cricket said, as they reached the school and Meg took over, leading the way to her grandparents' house. "It's just a matter of finding the stairs. Where did you look?"

"Everywhere," Meg replied. "I opened every door I could find. I looked in every closet. I even went over the walls to see if there might be a door cut into them. I don't see how—"

"Wait a second!" Cricket exclaimed. She stopped in the middle of the sidewalk and looked around.

"We're headed for Cascade Drive, aren't we? Is your grandparents' house one of those big old ones in the middle of the redwoods?"

"That's right," said Meg. "It's actually on Cascade Drive, just a few blocks from here. It's got two stories and lots of rooms and there's a—"

But Cricket didn't let her finish. "Did you look up?" she interrupted, grabbing Meg's arm excitedly.

"Up?" Meg repeated.

"At the ceiling," Cricket said.

Meg's face was blank.

"You didn't! Oh, Meg, I think I know where it is! And I know we can find it," Cricket said, starting to run. "Come on!"

C h a p t e r

By the time they reached her grandparents' house, Meg's heart was pounding and she was gasping for breath. She knocked on the door with the dolphin door knocker, but there was no answer.

"My grandmother's probably taken Kevin to the park," she said. "But don't worry, I know where there's a key." She picked up a pot of geraniums—third from the left—on the front porch, found the key that was hidden there, and unlocked the door.

Cricket stepped inside. "It's just as I thought!" she said, looking around. "A big front hall and a wide stairway. A friend of mine in first grade lived in one of these big old houses in the redwoods. *That's* why I think I know where the entrance to the attic is. Come on!" She dashed up the stairs to the second floor with Meg at her heels.

"Now, look up," she said. She tilted her head back

and peered up at the long narrow boards that ran the length of the ceiling above the second-floor hallway. "This is where it was in my friend's house," she explained. "There was a trapdoor cut right into the ceiling. You could hardly see it because the cuts were made between the boards. There was a metal ring that you pulled to open it and a stairway—kind of a slanted ladder—that slid down."

A door in the ceiling. Meg would never have thought of that! "No wonder I couldn't find it," she said, peering up at the boards with Cricket. The two of them walked the length of the hallway, heads tilted back, but they saw nothing that looked like a trapdoor.

"Maybe it's in another room," said Cricket, frowning. "I suppose you could put it anywhere—even in the bathroom."

They checked there first, but found nothing other than a spider web stretching from the overhead lamp to the top of the mirror. Next they looked in Meg's grandparents' big bedroom, then in the smaller room her mother was using, and in the tiny room where Kevin slept. By the time they got to Meg's bedroom, next door to Kevin's, Meg couldn't help feeling discouraged.

"I know there's nothing up there." She pointed to the boards above the bed. "I've spent hours staring at this ceiling, especially last night when I couldn't sleep. If there was a trapdoor I would have seen it," she said, beginning to suspect that maybe she'd been right—the secret attic was just her grandfather's idea of a joke!

"But it's got to be here," Cricket insisted. "If it's not in the ceiling . . ." She ran her hands over the wallboards, just as Meg had done that morning. Then she opened the door next to the big maple dresser. "Wow, this closet is huge," she said. "And dark. You don't suppose . . ."

Meg was one step ahead of her. She grabbed a flashlight from the night table drawer and shone it into the closet. She'd searched there earlier, looking for a door cut into the wall, but she hadn't been thinking about the ceiling then. Several zippered wardrobe bags, filled with clothes her grandmother couldn't bear to part with, hung from a rod at one end of the closet. Behind the bags was a large empty space. Meg had thought it was strange that nothing was stored back there. Now, with Cricket close behind, she pushed the wardrobe bags aside, stepped into the space, and shone the flashlight beam up.

And there it was!

"We found it!" Cricket exclaimed, looking at the clearly visible outline of a trapdoor cut into the boards of the ceiling. "There's the ring you pull to open it."

If Meg had been as tall as her grandfather, she could have reached right up and pulled on the ring. But a coat hanger would do just as well. Handing the flashlight to Cricket, she grabbed a metal hanger from the clothes rod and straightened it out. Then she hooked the curved end of the hanger into the ring and gave a sharp jerk. The trapdoor opened, and a ladderlike stair-way slid down, hitting the floor with a thud.

For a moment, neither girl spoke. The hazy light from the attic above bathed the closet in a ghostly glow. A fine shower of dust filtered down, sparkling in the beam of the flashlight that Cricket still held in her hand.

This must be what it's like to be an archaeologist, Meg thought. This must be how it feels to discover a hidden tomb, to creep down a secret passageway into a pyramid. She remembered what Cricket had said about skeletons, and though she knew her friend had been jok-ing, she couldn't help imagining a bony hand reaching down through the open doorway, a grinning skull, a dry cackle . . .

"Well, what are we waiting for?" said Cricket. The sound of her voice made Meg jump. Switching off the flashlight, she began to climb the stairs. Then suddenly she stopped. "No, wait," she said, stepping aside. "It's your attic. You go first."

Meg could see from the look in her eyes that Cricket would have loved to dash right up the stairs. But she was right. It *was* Meg's attic—or at any rate, her grandpar-ents' attic. The privilege belonged to her. Not that Meg was absolutely certain she wanted it, with the image of the skeleton looming in her mind. But she couldn't back down now.

Taking a deep breath, Meg started up the steps. There was no handrail, so she had to hold onto the stairs that rose steeply in front of her, extending her hand up into the unknown space above.

She heard a scratching sound. A rat? She'd seen a movie once where a girl was trapped in a closet with rats trying to chew their way through the walls to get at her. The thought of something skittering over her hand in the darkness made her shiver. The idea of a rat's scaly tail . . .

But that was nonsense! The scratching sound was probably made by a tree branch rubbing against the roof. She'd heard the same kind of sound outside her bedroom window whenever the wind blew. Getting a grip on herself, she continued to climb until her head, her shoulders, and the rest of her body passed through the trapdoor into the attic above.

She stood up, looked around the attic, and caught her breath in astonishment.

"What do you see?" Cricket called from down below. "What's up there?"

"What's *not* up here is more like it! My grandparents must have never thrown away anything," Meg said. "Come and see!"

That was all the invitation Cricket needed. She was up the stairs in a flash. "Ooh! I see what you mean!" she said.

The girls' eyes opened wide as they stared at the boxes and barrels, stacks of old magazines, suitcases, duffel bags, and trunks that were piled everywhere. And there was more. A quick glance around the room revealed an old rocking horse, a tricycle, an aquarium tank, a dog bed, an animal cage with an exercise wheel, an old toboggan, and skis. Spider webs crisscrossed the ceiling, which was low and slanted, just high enough at the center for Meg and Cricket to stand. A light bulb with a brass chain hung from the central rafter, but there was no need to turn it on. The round windows beneath the eaves, though streaked with dust, let in enough sunlight to bathe the attic in a hazy, yellowish glow.

"This is so strange," whispered Cricket, breaking the silence. "I feel like . . . like there's something up here."

"You mean a treasure?" Meg said, remembering what she'd been thinking earlier about finding an old baseball card collection. Looking at the jumble of old boxes and trunks that surrounded them, it certainly seemed possible.

"Maybe that," Cricket murmured. "Or maybe something else. Something bigger."

"Is this more of that kismet stuff?" Meg said. "Because if it is—"

"I know you don't believe in these things," Cricket interrupted her. "But I really do have a feeling that there's something up here that could change our lives!" She knelt down eagerly and wiped the dust off the nearest cardboard box until the words written in marking pen on the top were visible—*Income Tax Records: 1953*.

"Not exactly what you had in mind, is it?" Meg laughed, but it was a nervous laugh. In spite of herself, she couldn't help thinking that maybe Cricket was right. Maybe there was something hidden in the attic. Something important. But what?

Cricket laughed, too, as she read the words on the box. "Sorry. I don't mean to be so weird," she said. "I know I get carried away with things, but . . . Hey, look—" She broke off in the middle of her sentence. "I'll bet this is that box of photographs you're looking for." She dragged a carton, less dusty than the others, to the center of the floor. The words *Family Photos* were printed on the top.

This was more like it. Eagerly, Meg pulled back the lid. The box was filled almost to overflowing with photographs—old ones, new ones, black and white, and color. It was a regular treasure chest full of family history. Forgetting about Cricket's mysterious feelings, Meg dug into the box. In no time at all, she'd found a whole stack of baby pictures, including a few in which she had all her clothes on and didn't look too dorky. She figured she wouldn't mind putting one of those on the family bulletin board.

Cricket rummaged through the box with her. "There are some really old ones in here. I'll bet this is your grandmother," she said, holding out a small black-and-white snapshot of a girl in pigtails and an old-fashioned plaid dress. "And here's somebody's wedding picture."

"Mom and Dad," said Meg, taking the photo from her hand.

Cricket looked embarrassed. "Oh, I'm sorry," she murmured quickly. "I know you told me about your dad when we were talking the other day, but I forgot. I didn't mean to . . ."

"That's okay," Meg said. "Just because my father died doesn't mean I don't like to look at pictures of him. Actually, I was so young when it happened that pictures are really the only way I have to remember him." She looked at the photograph fondly.

Cricket nodded as if she understood. "Let's see what else we can find," she said, dumping the pictures she was holding back into the box. "Look. There's an old hamster cage. That should come in handy."

Meg dragged the box of photographs across the floor to the trapdoor so she'd remember to take it down with her. She couldn't wait to explore the rest of the attic. In no time at all, she'd found a cowboy hat, a pair of deer antlers, a box of old Christmas ornaments, a golf trophy, and a couple of fondue sets.

Cricket found a ukulele and the remains of a hula skirt. "And movie magazines!" she exclaimed. "From way back in the sixties. I'll bet they belonged to your mom."

"This must be hers, too," Meg said, dusting off a blue metal footlocker with the name *Janet* written on the side in what looked like red nail polish. A rusty lock hung from the hasp.

Cricket dropped the movie magazine and ran her hand over the footlocker. Meg saw a familiar expression come over her face.

"No, don't say it. You feel something. Right?"

"Maybe I do," said Cricket, fingering the lock. "Have you got something sharp, like a nail file?"

"I don't know if we should open it," Meg said. But she found herself handing Cricket a fork from one of the fondue sets and watching as she fitted the prongs into the keyhole. "Maybe we should get my mother's permission first." But it was too late. Cricket had wedged the fork in and given it a sharp turn. The rusty old lock popped open!

The trunk was packed so full that the top sprang up like a jack-in-the-box as soon as Cricket slipped the lock off the hasp. A stuffed elephant, a pink bunny, and a well-worn teddy bear with one ear and no eyes tumbled out onto the floor. There were dolls, too: a rag doll, a rubber doll, and one with a key in its back that must have done something a long time ago, but didn't seem to work anymore.

Cricket pulled out a tennis racket, rubber flippers, and a pennant that said *Camp Sequoia*. "That's interesting," she said. "I think my mother went to . . ."

But Meg wasn't listening. While Cricket had been pulling out sports equipment, she'd been rummaging in the bottom of the footlocker. Her eyes fell on something big and red. A photo album. No. A scrapbook. She hauled it out. As she looked at the cover, goose bumps popped out on her arms.

"Cricket, look at this," she said, pointing to the word printed in big bold letters on the red canvas cover. *SECRET!!* it said. Could this be what Cricket had felt? Beneath the word was a poem.

> *Beware, oh curious one*
> *For you may have to run*
> *If you dare to sneak a look*
> *Between the pages of this book!*

Meg and Cricket exchanged an excited glance. Should they do it? How could they not? Already Meg's fingers had slipped beneath the cover. Half-expecting the roof to collapse, a screeching ghost to appear, or poisonous fumes to envelop them, she held her breath—and opened the book.

Chapter

Nothing happened. The dry edges of the yellowed page cracked beneath Meg's fingers, fluttering away in a rain of brown flakes. But the roof didn't cave in, no evil spirits appeared.

Meg stared at the words that were printed in faded blue crayon at the center of the page. But she was too excited to take in what they meant. This was her mother's scrapbook—her *secret* scrapbook. How long had it lain at the bottom of the footlocker, beneath the stuffed animals, the flippers, the pennant from camp? What had she been thinking so many years ago when she'd picked up the blue crayon and written—

Meg's eyes finally focused on the writing. Suddenly it was as if the roof really *had* caved in. For there, printed in neat block letters, surrounded by a border of red hearts, were the words *ALWAYS FRIENDS*.

"Always Friends? Isn't that what's written on your teddy bear's T-shirt?" Cricket said.

Meg didn't trust herself to speak. She wasn't sure that she could. She felt the outline of the teddy bear that she'd tucked into the pocket of her new jeans from Baylor's. She could picture its T-shirt, the heart drawn by Jenny, the words written inside.

"Yes. Yes, it is," she said faintly.

"I knew it!" Cricket exclaimed. "I told you I had a feeling about this attic. It's kismet all over again! Turn the page." When Meg didn't move, she reached over and turned it herself.

The second page was as yellowed with age as the first. A border of stars was drawn around the edges and a sheet of notebook paper, covered with writing, was taped to the center. *Minutes of our very first meeting!* it said.

Minutes? A meeting? "It must have been a club!" Meg exclaimed, recovering her full voice. "The Always Friends Club." The words rolled off her tongue. What a perfect name for a club. But why hadn't her mother mentioned it? Meg was certain that she hadn't. It wasn't the sort of thing Meg would for-get—especially when Jenny had given her a bear with the very same words on its shirt.

Maybe her mother had forgotten about the club. Lots of things had happened to her since she was a girl. She'd gone to college, gotten married, had children, started a career. It wouldn't be surprising if she hadn't had much time to think about her childhood. Maybe the club was hidden somewhere deep in her memory, just as the scrapbook had been hidden deep in the bottom of her old blue footlocker.

"You know what I think," said Cricket, her voice bringing Meg back to the present. "I think we were meant to find this scrapbook. Because I think we were *meant* to start a club!"

"You mean like this one?"

"Exactly! Just listen to what it says here." Cricket pointed to the first paragraph of the minutes and read, " 'The goals of this club are to have fun, to help people, to earn money, and to always be friends.' Isn't that just what we were talking about today? Earning money and how hard it is for kids our age. But if we had a club . . ."

The excitement in her voice was catching. Maybe she was right. Maybe they *were* meant to find the scrapbook. In her mind, Meg heard an airplane landing, saw Jenny getting off. She leaned over the page and eagerly scanned the rest of the minutes. Someone named Linda had been chosen to come up with an idea for the club's first project, their goal was to earn $25, and the next meeting would be held at Judy's house. They voted to buy a scrapbook ("one of those nice big ones with the red covers that they sell at The Book Nook") and to treat themselves to hot fudge sundaes at Elmer's as soon as they had money in their treasury.

"Well, they got the scrapbook, so they must have

earned the money," Cricket said. "But how?"

The answer was on the very next page.

"A circus!" Meg exclaimed. "Just look at all this stuff."

Pasted across the double spread of pages beneath the headline OUR FIRST PROJECT—THE GREATEST SHOW ON EARTH was a dazzling array of colorful flyers, programs, and circus tickets, all of them decorated with hand-drawn pictures of acrobats, monkeys, and clowns. There were photographs, too.

"Great costumes!" said Cricket. She pointed to a photo of a chubby, blond-haired girl in a strongman's—a strong*woman's*—outfit, carrying a barbell made of a broom handle and two balloons. There was a gypsy fortune teller loaded with gold jewelry, a pair of clowns with frizzy orange hair and big noses, and someone dressed as a lion with a crepe paper mane.

On the next page were more photos. This time most of the girls wore T-shirts and jeans and seemed to be setting up the circus. "It looks like it was held right in the backyard of this house," Meg said. "That's my mom." She pointed to a photo of two girls standing together, their arms around each other's shoulders. One was wearing a clown mask. The other (Meg's mother) was grinning straight at the camera. Someone had written *Best Friends* above the picture and drawn a heart around it. "Look at how low that hedge is," she added, pointing to the row of neatly trimmed bushes behind the girls. "It's almost as tall as my grandfather now.

And there's no back porch on the house. They must have built that later when—" She broke off. "Cricket? What is it?" she said.

Cricket had suddenly leaped to her feet.

"What's the matter?"

But Cricket didn't reply. She headed for the trap-door. "I've got to go," she said, her face looking pale as she started down the stairs. "Wait here. Don't move. I'll be right back."

"But—" Meg dropped the scrapbook, rushed to the doorway, and peered into the closet below. But Cricket had already disappeared. She heard her footsteps pounding down the stairs to the first floor. "The bath-room's not down there, Cricket," she shouted, since that was the only reason she could think of for some-one to turn pale, say "I've got to go," and then dash away in such a hurry. "It's on the second floor."

There was no reply, but a moment later the front door slammed. Meg clambered over boxes and trunks to peer out of one of the round, dust-covered windows at the end of the attic. It overlooked the backyard, but Cricket was nowhere in sight. She tried the window at the other end. All she could see was one of the neigh-bors pruning his roses.

What was going on? Had Cricket had another of her feelings? Had she had a vision of her house burning down? Of her mother getting her apron caught in the food processor? Or was it something in the scrapbook?

Meg picked up the big red album from where she'd

dropped it by the footlocker. There was no point running after Cricket since she didn't know where she'd gone. Besides, now that she thought about it, she was sort of annoyed. She didn't like being ordered around. *Wait here. Don't move.* Who did Cricket think she was anyway? Jenny would never have done anything like that. She sat down on a duffel bag next to a stack of old *National Geographics.* If Cricket thought she was going to wait for her without looking at the scrapbook, she had another thing coming!

She opened the book to a different page. This time the blue-crayon headline at the top read OUR SECOND PROJECT—ALL THE LATEST FASHIONS FOR YOUR DOLLS. Beneath it were pasted sketches of clothes, scraps of fabric, and photos of all kinds of dolls—baby dolls, rag dolls, Barbies—dressed in beautiful clothes. On the next page was a newspaper clipping from the *Redwood Grove Daily News:* ENTERPRISING GIRLS OUTFIT LOCAL DOLLIES was the headline. Above it someone had written in orange crayon, *Fame at last!*

Forgetting all about Cricket, Meg turned eagerly from one page to another. What things these girls had done! They'd put on plays, washed windows, weeded gardens, given pony rides (Meg wondered who owned the pony), and even had a private-eye business! She didn't take time to read the minutes of their meetings or to look at the photos too closely. She was too busy turning pages, eager to find out what they'd done next.

How much money did they earn? she thought. Even if all their projects hadn't been as successful as the doll clothes that had been written up in the newspaper, it must have been a lot. Of course, it had to be divided. It looked like there had been four or five girls in the club. If they'd earned $25 and had to divide it five ways, then they'd have gotten just $5 each. That didn't seem like much—especially if you needed money for something big, like airfare from Los Angeles. But $5 must have gone further in those days. Hadn't her mother said you could even buy stuff for a nickel?

Meg wondered about the scrapbook itself. How much had it cost? Or those hot fudge sundaes the girls had bought at Elmer's to celebrate their first big success? They might have taken a picture while they were there, she thought. There might be a price list posted on the wall.

Quickly, Meg flipped through the scrapbook until she found a bunch of photos on the last page that didn't seem to fit anywhere else. There it was, a bit out of focus and faded with the years: five girls seated in a booth with enormous hot fudge sundaes in front of them. Meg squinted her eyes at the wall above the booth, hoping to find a price list. But there was only a poster for that old rock group The Beatles.

The girls certainly looked happy, whatever they'd paid for their sundaes. Meg's mother was right in the center, smiling a great big smile. A chubby, blond-haired girl—the one who'd been the strongwoman in the circus—was on one side of her, and on the other was a thin, freckle-faced girl. Her hair was curly, and might have been red, though the photo was so faded Meg couldn't really tell. She looked familiar. Of course she must have been in some of the other pictures in the scrapbook. Or maybe . . . Meg leaned closer to the picture.

"Meg!" A shout came from downstairs. "Are you still up there?" The front door slammed. Footsteps—Cricket's footsteps—pounded up the hall stairway.

"Where have you been?" Meg demanded, as Cricket climbed noisily up the secret stairs, through the trapdoor, and into the attic. Her cheeks were glowing and wisps of red hair were plastered damply to her forehead. She pressed her hand against her side as if she ached from running so fast.

"You are not going to believe this!" she exclaimed, ignoring the angry expression on Meg's face. "Give me the scrapbook."

"Now wait a second," Meg objected. She wasn't about to let Cricket start ordering her around again!

But Cricket paid no attention. She grabbed the scrapbook from Meg's hands and sank down on the duffel bag. Quickly she flipped through the pages to the circus photos they'd been looking at before she left. Then she reached into her shirt pocket and pulled out a faded photograph. Its edges were torn, as if it had been ripped from an album by someone in too much of a hurry to be careful. "Look!" she said, placing her photo next to the photo in the scrapbook—the one with a heart drawn around it.

Meg looked. Then she looked again, not quite believing what she saw. They were the same! Cricket's photo and the photo in the scrapbook—the photo with *Best Friends* written above it—were exactly the same!

"But I don't understand," Meg said. "How—"

"I found this last night," Cricket said breathlessly, "when I was going through our old photo albums. It says, 'Me as a clown' on the back. See?" She turned the photo over. "That's my mother's writing. And this is *her*," she said, turning the photo over again and pointing to the girl in the clown mask. "*That's* my mother!"

"But . . ." Meg's mind struggled to make sense out of what her eyes were telling her. "But that's *my* mother," she said, pointing to the other girl in the photo. She thought of the picture taken at Elmer's. Now she knew who the girl sitting next to her mother looked like. She grabbed the album from Cricket and flipped to the last page. "That's her, isn't it?" she said, pointing at the picture.

Cricket nodded. She looked as if she didn't trust herself to speak. "Yes. It's my mother," she said finally, staring at the picture of the freckle-faced girl sitting beside Meg's mother. "She grew up in Redwood Grove, but she had to move to Oregon because her father got a job there. Her name was Karen Parker then, before she married my dad and became Karen Connors, and—Oh, Meg!"

The girls looked at each other. The attic was still. The tree branches had stopped scraping against the roof. Meg felt as if they were tumbling through time, back to that booth in Elmer's Ice Cream Emporium. She could hear Cricket breathing beside her. She could practically smell the hot fudge.

Then all at once someone shouted, "Meg? Kevin?" It was Mrs. Kelly, calling from downstairs. "I'm home. Is anybody here?"

The girls flew down the secret stairway, Meg first, scrapbook in hand, with Cricket close behind. They pushed past the wardrobe bags in the closet, tore through Meg's bedroom, and raced into the upstairs hallway. They were halfway down the stairs when the telephone in the front hall began to ring. Mrs. Kelly answered it.

"Hello. Yes. This is Meg's mother," she said. She glanced up to see the girls practically tumbling down the stairs. "Why, yes, she's right here. A bit out of breath, I think, but . . ." She held out the receiver to Cricket. "It's your mother," she said.

"Oh, Mom! No, it's not!" Meg exclaimed. "I mean it is, but it's not just Cricket's mother. It's Karen! Karen Parker. Your best friend!"

Chapter

After that, so many things happened so fast that Meg could barely keep up with them.

First, Cricket took the phone and began telling her mother, in a torrent of words, about the attic and the scrapbook and the pictures. While she was talking, Meg told her mother about discovering the secret stairway and opening the footlocker. She showed her the scrapbook and then Cricket's photo. Finally, after a lot of "You did what?" and "She's really who?" both of the mothers began to understand. Then things really got hectic.

Mrs. Kelly sank down on the hall stairs, the phone gripped so tightly in her hand that her knuckles were white. "Karen! Karen Parker," she kept repeating. "I can't believe it. I just can't believe it!" Cricket's mother was saying the same kinds of things on the other end of the line.

In the middle of it all, Meg's grandmother and Kevin came home from the park, followed shortly by her grandfather returning from his birdwatching trip. And then everything had to be explained all over again.

"Invite her to dinner," Grandpa urged. "I remember that girl was always interested in eating."

Cricket's mother accepted immediately. Then Meg's grandmother picked up the phone to find out why Mrs. Connors had never looked them up. It turned out that she'd tried, but the year she'd moved back to Redwood Grove, with Cricket and Cricket's father, was the same year Meg's grandparents had rented out the big old house in the redwoods and moved to New York. By the time they returned, several years later, Mrs. Connors had given up on finding them. She assumed that they'd moved away for good.

"Amazing," Grandma said, shaking her head as she handed the phone back to Meg's mother. "To think that she was here all along. Little Karen Parker. Why, I may have passed her in the street without even knowing it. I suppose she's a good deal bigger now, though. And I may be just a tad older-looking, too," she added.

"But still just as lovely," said Grandpa gallantly. "Now let's go show this young man the attic." He took Kevin, who'd been making impatient noises for the last half hour, by the hand. "Then we can lay down a few rules about who can go up there and when."

Fortunately, everyone was too excited to be angry at Meg and Cricket for exploring the attic, breaking open the footlocker, and reading the secret scrapbook on their own. In fact, just the opposite was true. Their mothers couldn't thank them enough!

"It's like a miracle, isn't it?" said Mrs. Connors. They'd finished dinner—a noisy, laughter-filled meal—and she and Meg's mother were seated on the sofa in the living room, with Meg and Cricket beside them and the scrapbook spread out on their laps. Meg's grandmother was upstairs putting Kevin to bed, and her grandfather was in the kitchen loading the dishwasher. He'd been so impressed by the tofu and eggplant stew that Mrs. Connors had insisted on bringing for dinner that, much to Meg's relief, he'd made her promise to give him cooking lessons!

"I'm so sorry Dave couldn't make it tonight," Mrs. Connors said. Dave was Cricket's father. "He's dying to meet you. But he just couldn't miss that school board meeting."

"I know I'm going to like him," said Mrs. Kelly. "It seems so incredible, though, you with a husband."

"And both of us mothers! I can't believe how much we have to catch up on. I'll never forgive myself for not keeping up after I moved, but—"

"Mom," Cricket interrupted. "Save the apologies for later. We want to know about the club!"

"Yes!" Meg said. She'd heard enough over dinner about how time flew and what a small world it was. Somewhere between the salad and the dessert she'd begun to accept things. And by the time the table was cleared, it seemed like the most natural thing in the world that her mother and Cricket's mother had been best friends. But the club was what mattered now. "We want to know everything," she said. "Who was in it, how it got started . . ."

"How much money you made," Cricket chimed in.

"Hmm. Do I detect the beginnings of a new club here?" Mrs. Connors said with a smile. "Well, let me see . . . I guess it started out like any club does. A bunch of friends get together and they're bored and someone says, 'Hey, why don't we have a club.' "

"That's right," Mrs. Kelly agreed. "But it didn't really get going until we read that book. Remember, Karen? What was its name?"

"*The Saturdays*. How could I ever forget," said Mrs. Connors. "Oh, it was wonderful. All about a family of kids—two boys and two girls—who get tired of never having enough from their allowances to do anything special. So they decide to pool their money, and each week one of them gets to spend the entire amount. Remember, Janet, how Mona—she was the oldest girl—got a permanent and a manicure?"

"And how Oliver went to tea with that wealthy lady, Mrs. Olliphant," laughed Meg's mother. "And how Randy—"

"Mom, stop!" Meg interrupted, afraid that if they began sharing memories again, there'd be no end to it. "We don't want to know about some old book. We want to know how *your* club worked."

"Ah, yes," said her mother. "Sorry for getting side-tracked, but that book is where we got the idea for the money-making part of our club. We didn't use our allowances like they did, though. What we did was choose one girl to think up a project. It had to be fun, and it had to have the possibility of earning money or helping people—preferably both. Then we'd do the project, and if it earned money—as I remember it had to be at least twenty-five dollars—we'd put our names into a hat and the girl whose name was drawn got to spend the money."

"Of course, that sometimes caused bad feelings," Cricket's mother said. "If a girl really wanted money for something and her name wasn't drawn, she might be put out. But it seemed the only fair way to do things. Once your name got drawn, you couldn't put it in again, so eventually everyone got a turn."

So that was how it worked! "I had it all wrong," said Meg. "I thought you just divided the money up, so if you earned twenty-five dollars, you'd get five dollars each. But that didn't seem like much."

"Twenty-five dollars isn't much, either," Cricket pointed out. She couldn't help sounding disappointed. "I mean, it's more than five dollars, but still . . ."

"Oh, but it was a lot in those days," said her mother. "Considering what things cost, I'd say twenty-five dollars then was about the same as one hundred dollars today. Wouldn't you, Janet?"

That started them off again, talking about how

cheap Popsicles and comic books and movie tickets had been. But Meg hardly heard. One hundred dollars! She looked at Cricket and knew they were thinking the same thing. They could do it. They would do it!

"Tomorrow," Cricket said, when Mrs. Connors had finally declared it was time to go home and they were all saying good night in the hall. "We'll tell Amy— she's got to be a part of this—and then we'll make plans!"

Meg could *not* fall asleep. If it had been difficult last night, when she'd just found out about the secret attic, it was impossible tonight. She lay in her bed and stared up at the ceiling. Only a thin layer of boards separated her from the shadowy world of the attic above with its stacks of old magazines, sports trophies, tax records, and the footlocker where she'd found the secret scrapbook.

She thought of the big red album, now lying on the coffee table in the living room. Once they started their club—she and Cricket and Amy—they'd have to keep a scrapbook, too. She wondered if The Book Nook was still in business. Did they sell scrapbooks with red canvas covers? They'd need a notebook, too, for taking minutes of their meetings. And they'd have to find a camera to use for taking photos. But what kind of projects could they do?

Meg turned on her side so she could stare out the window at the redwood trees silhouetted in the moonlight. That was a good question. Were there as many ways to earn money now as there had been when their mothers were young? It seemed like there might be a lot more competition. You could buy all kinds of gorgeous doll clothes from toy stores and catalogs. And would anyone come to a backyard circus to see someone dressed up as a lion when they could see real ones any night on TV?

"Meg?" The door opened a crack, letting in a shaft of light from the hall. Her mother peeked in. "Are you asleep?"

"How could I be? I've got so many things going on in my head, I'll probably never sleep again!" Meg said.

"I know what you mean," her mother agreed. She slipped inside and sat down on the bed. "I brought you some hot milk." She set the mug she was carrying down on the night table. "Maybe it will help. It's been quite an evening, hasn't it?"

And quite a day, Meg thought, taking a sip of milk and remembering all that had happened even *before* they found the secret scrapbook. Seeing Pete's grave, meeting Cricket's mother, to say nothing of spying on Brittany in the stationery store. So many things had happened, all that seemed like a lifetime ago!

She looked at her mother, still dressed in her Savvy Lady suit, and remembered something else. "Mom, this was your first day at work. I almost forgot," she said. "How did it go?"

"Oh, all right, I guess." Mrs. Kelly sighed. "The

people are nice, but . . ." A worried look came over her face.

"What?" Meg said. "Is something wrong?" She imagined someone laughing at her mom's new suit. But grown-ups didn't do things like that . . . did they?

"Not exactly. It's just that I've been stuck with a difficult assignment," Mrs. Kelly replied. "I have to set up a focus group for this Saturday. Someone else was supposed to do it, but she's been out sick. So even though I'm brand-new it's up to me to—"

"Wait. Back up," Meg interrupted. "What's a focus group?"

"Oh, sorry." Her mother laughed. "Here I am just one day on the job and already I'm speaking another language. A focus group is a group of people—ordinary customers—that a company brings in to get some feedback about the products they're developing. In this case, it's a new computer game the company's designing. It's sort of like that one you were trying out yesterday."

Meg remembered. That was the game where a daring hero had to rescue some stupid princess who sat around in a tower looking helpless.

"What I have to do is get together a group of four boys about your age and bring them in on Saturday to play the game and talk with the designers and programmers," Mrs. Kelly said. "The trouble is I don't know any boys around here! I suppose I can ask at your school tomorrow. Ms. Uchida might be able to help me. It's short notice, but since the boys will be paid twenty-five dollars each for participating . . ."

Meg nearly dropped the mug of milk she was holding. Four boys at $25 each. That was $100! But why did they have to be boys? "Mom!" she exclaimed. "You don't have to ask at my school. You've got your focus group right here. You've got us—me and Cricket and Amy!"

"But you're—" Her mother stopped herself.

"I know, we're girls. But half the kids in this country are girls and they like computers. I bet they'd like them even more if so many of the games weren't made just for boys!"

Mrs. Kelly looked at Meg as if she were seeing her for the very first time. "How did you get so smart?" she said. "Why didn't I think of that? It's exactly what this company needs. Instead of competing with other companies for the same group of boys, they could design games that would attract new customers—including girls. This focus group could be just what they need to get them thinking in a new direction."

"Then we can do it?" Meg said.

"As far as I'm concerned, yes," replied her mother. "I'll have to check with my boss, but I think he'll agree. He hired me because he wants new ideas," she said, her eyes shining, the worried look gone from her face. "Now if only I had someone who could speak French."

"French?" Meg repeated. Though she said the

word, for a moment it didn't quite register in her mind. She was too excited. They had their first project! It wouldn't come to $100 because there were just three of them, but still . . . She stopped. All of a sudden the word sank in. "Wait a second," she said. "Mom, did you say you need someone who speaks French?"

Mrs. Kelly nodded. "It's another little problem of mine. One of the programmers who's working on this game is from France. He'll be sitting in on this focus group. He's brilliant, but I'm afraid he only speaks French so we'll have trouble communicating. It certainly would be nice if—"

But Meg didn't let her go on. "Mom!" she interrupted excitedly. "Don't worry." She didn't know what Amy and Cricket would say, but she didn't care. Her mother was going to make a terrific impression at her new company and *she* was going to help. "You're going to have a great focus group, Mom," she said. "I guarantee it. You'll have four girls—and one of those girls will speak French!"

C h a p t e r

Me?" Brittany Logan said. Her thickly lashed eyes opened wide as she stared at Meg in astonishment. "You want me? But . . . but I don't understand."

Meg hesitated. She'd arrived at school early and waited outside for the school bus, hoping to have a chance to talk to Brittany before Cricket and Amy showed up. But she'd been so worried about convincing the two of them to include Brittany that she hadn't given much thought to convincing Brittany herself! Now here they were, standing at the bottom of the school steps with kids hurrying past them and she had no idea what to answer.

"Well, like I said, it's a focus group," she repeated lamely, "at my mother's company."

"Oh, I understood that part," said Brittany. "What I meant is, why me? I don't know much about computers and . . . and I haven't been very . . . Please, Meg," she said, her cheeks coloring slightly as she used Meg's name for the very first time. "You must forgive me for what I said about the car. It's just that . . ."

"Oh, that's okay," Meg said, glad to have a chance to change the subject. "You probably weren't feeling well. That was the day you got sick." She watched Brittany's face for a reaction.

"Well, I wasn't *very* sick," said Brittany quickly, not looking Meg in the eye. "But about the limousine . . . you see, it's sort of embarrassing. It's only temporary, though. My father's company gave it to him for a month for commuting to the airport. He has to fly around the country a lot until he gets settled here. My mother uses it, too, because she's opening a branch of her company in San Francisco and—" She stopped, as if overwhelmed by the effort of making such a lengthy speech.

Meg felt sorry for her. Maybe Cricket was right. Maybe it *was* hard being rich. Maybe having a father who spent his time commuting to the airport in a limousine and flying around the country, and a mother with businesses in Paris and New York—and now San Francisco—wasn't so easy.

"She's Adrienne Logan, isn't she?" said Meg. "Your mother, I mean." She pulled Brittany's jacket out of the shopping bag she was carrying and handed it to her. "You left this on your chair and I noticed the label," she explained. She didn't mention spying on her in the stationery store.

Brittany blushed again. "Oh. Thank you," she murmured. "I get to wear a lot of the clothes my mother designs—mostly samples that are made in a small size. But what I really like . . ." She glanced at Meg hesitantly. "What I really like," she said, "are things like that sweater you're wearing. Did you get it around here?"

"This?" Meg liked her new blue cable knit, too, but it was hardly in the same league as the gorgeous jade green sweater set Brittany was wearing. "Uh, yes. I got it at Baylor's," she replied, finding it hard to believe that she was giving fashion advice to someone whose mother was a famous designer. "They're having a . . ." But Brittany Logan would hardly be interested in a sale!

"Baylor's," Brittany repeated. "Maybe I can go there. And . . . and I would like to be in this focus group," she added earnestly. "That is, if you're sure you really want me."

Meg hoped that the guilt she felt creeping over her didn't show on her face. If Brittany—who suddenly seemed so human, so vulnerable, so likable even—found out that the only reason Meg was asking her to be part of the group was because she spoke French . . . But she didn't even want to think about it. She didn't want to think that she, Meg Kelly, was that sort of a person!

"Of course I want you," she declared. "That's why I'm asking you. Cricket Connors and Amy Chan will be doing it, too. My mother will take us there on Saturday morning. She'll call your parents to explain things and get their permission. And we'll be paid twenty-five dollars each," she added. She didn't think that would make much difference to Brittany Logan. But she was wrong.

"Twenty-five dollars!" Brittany exclaimed. Her eyes lit up. "*Ah c'est tres* . . . I mean, that's wonderful! I don't have much money."

Meg looked at her in disbelief. "You don't?" she said.

"No. Not of my own," Brittany replied. "My parents are very strict that way. I get the tiniest allowance and I have to do chores. Not that I'm complaining," she added quickly. "They've been very kind to me, so . . ." Her voice trailed off.

Kind to me? What sort of thing was that to say about your parents? Meg thought. It sounded strange. But maybe it was just the way kids talked about their parents in France.

"Well . . . thank you," said Brittany awkwardly. "I guess I'll see you Saturday morning then." She started up the steps. Meg wanted to reach out and stop her. She glanced at the crowd of kids hurrying into the school, looking for Cricket and Amy. But they were nowhere to be seen.

Suddenly, looking at Brittany's slender figure climbing the steps, remembering the surprise in her voice as she'd said, "You want me?" Meg knew what she had to do. Cricket and Amy might be angry, they might say she was nuts, but she couldn't let Brittany go.

"Brittany, wait!" she called, catching up at the entrance to the school. "I almost forgot. We're having a sleepover Friday night—Cricket and Amy and me. Can you come?"

Brittany looked shocked. "A sleepover? You're asking *me* to a sleepover?"

"Yes," said Meg, almost as surprised as Brittany was. "It's supposed to be at Amy's house, but maybe we'll change it to mine. That way we'll all be there and ready to go to the focus group Saturday morning. Can you come?" she repeated.

"Are you kidding!" exclaimed Brittany, sounding like an ordinary kid for the very first time. "I'd absolutely love to!"

Cricket and Amy weren't as easy to convince. They arrived together just after Brittany had thanked Meg again and disappeared into the building. "I can't believe it!" said Amy, as they joined Meg on the front steps. "I go away for one day and the two of you find a hidden attic, discover a secret scrapbook, and realize that you're practically sisters. It's not fair!"

"But you'll get in on the good stuff," Cricket said. "Won't she, Meg? We'll have that sleepover Friday night, and think up some great projects to do."

That's when Meg told them about the focus group. And when they got done exclaiming about that, she told them about Brittany.

"Wait a second. Am I hearing right?" said Amy. "Brittany Logan at a sleepover at my house? You've got to be kidding!"

Even Cricket had doubts. "I can see why you want her in the focus group," she said. "But how about the club? If she comes to the sleepover, we won't even be able to talk about it."

Meg hadn't thought about that. "I don't know," she replied. "All I know is it felt wrong not to invite her. And the sleepover doesn't have to be at your house, Amy. It can be at mine. That way we'll be ready to leave Saturday morning. Brittany's not the kind of person you think she is. If you just talked to her . . ."

"But I tried," Amy said, as the morning bell started to ring.

"Then maybe you should try again," Meg said angrily.

"Well, if *that's* the way you're going to be . . ." Amy made a face and stormed into the school.

Cricket tried to smooth things over, but it wasn't easy. Amy sulked for a few days, then got tired of it. But she still didn't try to talk to Brittany. Brittany, sensing that something was wrong, retreated into her shell. And Meg, caught in the middle, felt like some sort of criminal.

By the time Friday night came, the girls—Meg and Cricket and Amy—had agreed on only one thing. They would *not* mention the Always Friends Club to Brittany. She could take the $25 she earned from the focus group and do whatever she wanted with it. Then the three of them would go to Elmer's to celebrate and make plans for the club.

It sounded easy, but Meg couldn't help feeling *un*easy. She wished that Jenny were here. She was good at bringing people together and working out differences. As it was, all Meg could think of to do was to keep herself busy, helping Grandpa with the pizza he was making for the sleepover (using a recipe from Mrs. Connors, thank goodness), setting up the stereo in her room, and listening to Kevin chatter about the Winnie-the-Pooh book his teacher was reading in nursery school. The first guest arrived just in time to save her from hearing for the umpteenth time about how Pooh had gotten stuck in Rabbit's hole.

It was Amy. "I wanted to get here early so I could see if Miss Money Bags comes in her limousine," she said, dumping her sleeping bag in the hall.

Meg bit her tongue. She was *not* going to get into a fight with Amy.

Cricket showed up next, carrying her sleeping bag and a big carrot cake. "Your grandpa's going to love this. It's made with strained prunes instead of butter. Don't make a face," she said. "It's really delicious."

Brittany arrived last. *Not* in the limousine, but in a silver-gray sports car driven by her father. Mrs. Kelly went out to meet him, while Meg brought Brittany, dressed in a sweatshirt and jeans that might have come from Baylor's, into the house.

"What a wonderful place this is," Brittany said politely, stepping into the front hall and looking around appreciatively.

"We like it," said Meg's grandmother, coming out to greet her with Kevin in tow. "I'm glad you could come. Meg's grandfather is just putting the pizza together."

"I get to watch a video. *The Jungle Book*," Kevin announced.

"Me, too," said Grandma. "Kevin and I are buddies tonight. Now why don't you girls take your sleeping bags upstairs to Meg's room. We'll let you know when the pizza's ready."

Brittany's face fell. "Sleeping bags?" she repeated, as Kevin dragged Grandma away to the kitchen. Meg suddenly noticed that though she had a tote bag slung over her shoulder—an elegant black one with *Musée de Pompidou* printed on the side—she had no quilted bag with pictures of Mickey Mouse (like Amy's) or rain forest scenes (like Cricket's) tucked under her arm.

"Didn't you bring one?" Cricket asked.

"It *is* a sleepover, you know," said Amy.

"Uh . . . n-no," Brittany stammered. "I didn't realize. You see, I've never . . ."

The girls exchanged a glance. Was she going to say that she'd never been to a sleepover?

"That's okay," Meg said, coming to her rescue. "My grandparents have lots of extra bags. They go camping all the time. They're loaning me one for tonight, too. Now come on." She took Brittany's tote bag from her shoulder and started up the stairs. "We'll stick all this stuff in my room. Then we can try out a few games on the computer. Sort of get psyched up for tomorrow, you know."

Things went a lot better after that. Brittany gratefully took the sleeping bag Meg offered her and they all trooped back downstairs to the study to turn on the computer. Playing the games turned out to be a terrific idea (worthy of Jenny, Meg thought, feeling pleased with herself). Amy was happy because she was good at them. She scored highest in the game where you had to rescue the princess. No one else could zap monsters faster than she could. But Brittany, who at first didn't even seem to know what a mouse was, surprised everyone by coming out the winner in another game that involved solving math puzzles.

Even Amy was impressed. "How do you do that?" she said admiringly, as Brittany keyed in the answer to a puzzle that the rest of them had been struggling to solve.

"I don't know," Brittany admitted, blushing slightly. "I've always been good with numbers. The answer just sort of comes to me."

"Well, I wish it would come to me," said Amy. She eyed Brittany thoughtfully. "I'll bet you're good at cards, too," she said. "Do you play hearts?"

Brittany's eyes lit up. "Oh, yes," she replied. "In my school last year we played all the time."

"You played cards in school?" Meg was surprised. What kind of school would let kids play cards all the time? Before she could ask, Kevin burst into the study.

"The pizza's ready!" he said. "Grandpa says come and get it before he eats it all up! It's good this time, too," he whispered to Meg.

Meg knew he was remembering the pizza Grandpa had made the night they arrived—something with oat bran, cottage cheese, and kale. Mrs. Connors's recipe was a definite improvement!

The girls took bites and praised the cook, then carried the rest upstairs, along with apple juice and carrot cake, to Meg's room. They spread a checked tablecloth on the floor. Meg popped a new Pony Boys tape that Cricket had brought over into the stereo. She turned up the volume. They might as well play it loud, at least for the five minutes it would take before her mom came running up the stairs to complain.

"I just love them," Cricket shouted to Brittany, as the music burst out, rattling the windows and pounding their eardrums. "Don't you?"

"I don't know," Brittany shouted back. "Who are they?"

"The Pony Boys! Only the hottest group around," Cricket replied, as Meg lowered the volume to save her mother a trip upstairs. "Don't tell me you haven't heard of them."

"Oh. Oh, The Pony Boys! Of course." Brittany nodded. But no one was fooled.

Meg and Cricket exchanged a glance.

"Brittany," Amy said seriously, "where have you been?" She wasn't being sarcastic. She really wanted to know—who was Brittany Logan?

Brittany lowered her eyes, and her cheeks turned red. She looked as if she wanted to disappear.

"Come on, Brittany," Meg urged, turning off the tape. "It's not fair. You know who we are, but we don't know anything about you, except that your mother's a fashion designer and your father's got a limousine and you speak—I mean—" She caught herself just in time. "I mean, fill us in," she said. "Start with your school. It sounds great to go to a school where you can play cards all day."

"Oh, we didn't play during the school day," Brittany said. "Just in the evenings and on weekends. It was a boarding school. In Switzerland."

"No kidding!" Amy looked impressed. "I never knew anyone who went to boarding school. But didn't you miss your parents?"

"Of course, I did," said Brittany. "But they were both so busy last year. They had to travel a lot. That's why we moved to Redwood Grove," she added. "My mother wants us to settle down and have a more ordinary life."

"Well, I guess you can't get more ordinary than this," Cricket laughed. "Look at us, pigging out on pizza and listening to The Pony Boys. I hope your mother doesn't get too ordinary, though," she added.

"She's so elegant-looking. I can't imagine my mother ever dressing like—" She stopped herself, but not in time.

"You mean you've seen my mother?" Brittany said suspiciously. "But where? She hasn't come to school. She's hardly been in town except for the other day when . . ." Her voice trailed off nervously.

Meg looked at Cricket. Should they come clean? She didn't want to tell Brittany they'd been spying on her, but it seemed like they had to say something. "Uh . . . well . . . we were in the stationery store the other day when you and your mother came in," she said. There was no need to mention that they'd followed Brittany in! "You were buying a picture frame."

"That's right. A plastic one with a picture of a baby in it," Cricket said, not seeming to notice the expression that had come over Brittany's face. "Your mother was wearing the most gorgeous—"

"Cricket," Meg warned.

But it was too late. Brittany's lower lip was trembling. Her huge blue-gray eyes had turned dark. "You . . . you saw," she said. "The picture . . ." And then, covering her face with her hands, her tawny blond hair tumbling over her shoulders, she burst into tears.

C h a p t e r

Meg didn't know what to do.

"Well, don't just sit there," said Amy, leaping up from her place at the other side of the tablecloth. She stepped over the pizza and knelt down beside Brittany. "Get her a Kleenex." She put an arm around Brittany's shoulder and gave her a shake. "Hey, it's okay," she said, a bit gruffly. "I'd feel bad, too, if I thought someone was spying on me."

"You'd feel bad?" Cricket exclaimed. "But you were the one who—"

"Oh, please, don't fight," Brittany moaned. "It's not that I think anyone was spying on me. It's . . ." She took the Kleenex Meg thrust into her hand. "It's the picture."

"The picture? You mean the frame?" Meg said, feeling confused. Surely all this sobbing wasn't because she wished she'd gotten the silver frame instead of the plastic one!

"No, I mean the picture. The picture *in* the frame," Brittany said, tears welling up in her eyes again. "That's what I wanted. The picture of the baby—for the family bulletin board."

For a moment, Meg didn't know what she was talking about. Then, all at once, she understood. Brittany was in the same fix she was! She'd just moved to Redwood Grove, her things were packed away, and she didn't have a baby picture. She'd certainly picked a strange way to solve her problem, but still . . . "Brittany, don't worry," she said. "Not having a picture for the bulletin board is nothing to get so upset about. I had the same problem. All my baby pictures were in storage, so—"

"No. No, you don't understand," Brittany interrupted. "I don't have any baby pictures anywhere. I don't know anything about myself as a baby. My parents got me when I was two years old. From an orphanage."

An orphanage? The girls looked at Brittany in astonishment. They knew about kids who were adopted, of course, and kids who'd lived in foster homes. But an orphanage sounded like something out of a novel.

"I don't remember anything about it because I was so young," Brittany went on, the words tumbling out of her mouth, as if she'd been wanting to say them for a long, long time. "It was in France. After my parents adopted me, we moved to New York—that's where they're from—then back to France. And to

Switzerland. I . . . I haven't had a very ordinary life," she finished, blowing her nose loudly.

For a moment, no one said anything because no one could think of anything to say. Finally, Amy, who still had her arm around Brittany's shoulder, cleared her throat and declared, "You know what, Brittany, you could be anyone—a princess, or the heir to a kingdom. I saw a movie once about a woman who was the long-lost daughter of a Russian czar who'd—"

"Amy," Cricket interrupted, "stop it. She knows who she is. She knows who her parents are. She's living with them right now. They chose her because they wanted her. That's what it means to be adopted. Right, Brittany?"

"I . . . I guess so," said Brittany. "I hadn't really thought of it like that. They're always so busy . . . "

"But they moved to Redwood Grove to have a more ordinary life. Your mother said so, right? That means they're probably going to try not to be so busy," said Cricket. "Parents can change, you know, just like kids can."

Brittany was silent for awhile, as if she were thinking—hard. Then she wiped her eyes with the back of her hand and blew her nose again. "I'm sorry," she said, shaking her head. "I know this is stupid. I knew as soon as I got that picture that I'd never be able to bring it to class. Then when you said that you'd seen me in the stationery store, everything seemed to fall apart. I've been trying so hard to fit in, but . . . but I just don't know how to do things, and . . . Oh, this is so embarrassing!"

"No, it's not," said Meg, pouring her a glass of apple juice while Cricket handed her a piece of cake. "That's what friends are for. To listen to each other's problems, to help each other out."

"That's right," said Amy. "Maybe you just haven't had friends before."

Brittany looked as if she were going to break down in tears all over again. "Oh, that's so kind of you," she said. "You don't know how much it meant when you invited me here, Meg. The idea that you wanted me just because . . . well, just because I'm me!"

Meg was glad that Kevin showed up at just that moment.

"I'm not supposed to be here," he announced, bursting into the room. "I'm supposed to stay out of your hair. But I wanted to tell you that you can come and watch *The Jungle Book* with Grandma and me. We can have popcorn!"

Suddenly, having popcorn and watching a video with Kevin was exactly what everyone wanted to do. "Hooray!" Kevin shouted, tearing down the stairs to tell Grandma. Brittany blew her nose one last time. Amy picked up the pizza, while Cricket scooped up the carrot cake. Meg, feeling as if she'd discovered the earth beneath her feet was quicksand, gathered up the drinks and followed the others downstairs.

The VCR was set up in the family room. The opening music was already playing and goofy animal characters were frolicking across the screen. Meg's grandmother, seated on the sofa with Kevin, looked up with a smile when the girls appeared. She patted the space beside her and held out her hand to Brittany. "Oh," Brittany said. Looking as if she'd been offered the crown jewels, she sank down on the sofa beside her.

Meg and Cricket and Amy hesitated in the doorway. "We've got to talk," Amy whispered, saying what all of them were thinking. Mumbling something about going to get the popcorn, they retreated to the kitchen.

"What are we going to do?" said Cricket, putting the carrot cake down on the counter. "She's *got* to be in the club, but we can't tell her now. It'll seem like . . . well, like what it is," she said dismally.

"Maybe we should just tell the truth," Amy suggested. "Until tonight she wasn't someone we wanted to have in a club with us, and now she is. What's wrong with that?"

"Everything," Meg groaned. "It'll make her feel awful." It'll make *me* look awful was what she was thinking. "Why don't we just do what we planned. I already told my mother not to say anything about Brittany speaking French because it would make her feel self-conscious. So when she speaks French in the focus group, it'll seem natural, like it just happened. Later, we can all go to Elmer's—Brittany, too—and talk about starting a club. We'll make it sound like it's something we just thought up."

"But we didn't," said Cricket. "We found the attic and the scrapbook. The whole thing is based on our mothers' club. We can't lie about that."

"But it's not a lie. It's just . . ."

"Not the truth," said Amy, who was good at summing things up.

Meg was saved from having to reply by Brittany, who suddenly appeared in the doorway. "What's going on in here? Can I help?" she asked, not seeming to notice the awkward silence that had fallen over the girls. "Kevin put the video on pause so you wouldn't miss anything. He's so sweet," she said happily, picking up the big bowl of popcorn that Meg's grandfather had left for them on the kitchen table. "You know what he said, Meg? That he'd hold my hand when the movie got scary. Isn't that cute?"

It was. Once again, Meg couldn't help thinking that when you were Kevin's age, life was a lot easier!

Meg was glad there was no more time for talking, and it seemed that Cricket and Amy were, too. At any rate, they were certainly eager to head back to the family room to watch the video. Kevin, who'd seen *The Jungle Book* a zillion times already, told the girls everything that was going to happen before it happened and held Brittany's hand during the scary parts just as he'd promised.

By the time the movie was over and the popcorn bowl was empty, the memory of the conversation in the kitchen was beginning to fade. And by the time the girls woke up the next morning, after a night of giggling and ghost stories, the whole thing had begun to seem like a dream. When they got to the computer software company, no one was thinking about anything except what kind of games they would play.

"This is so exciting," said Amy as Meg's mother led them into the testing room. The light was low to minimize glare. Computer screens glowed from every table and desk. "My brothers are green with envy," she said. "They'd love to work as testers in a company like this."

"Well, maybe they can some day," said Mrs. Kelly. "We hire lots of people to play the games as they're being developed. Playing them is the only way to catch glitches or bugs in the software."

She left to talk to her boss, while one of the testers set the girls up, each at her own computer, and demonstrated the games they were going to play. He passed out notepads and pencils for them to jot down questions and ideas. "These games aren't finished yet, so you won't be able to play them through to the end," he explained. "But do the best you can. Then we'll get together with the programmers and the product manager to find out what you think of them. Okay? Go to it!" he said.

For the next hour, the girls were glued to their computers, pointing and clicking, typing on the keyboards, making the animated characters do all sorts of things on the screen. Meg thought the games were fun, especially one where you went through a maze and heard tunes played on various instruments. She could think of ways to make them better, though. She also thought of new kinds of games she wished they would make.

By the time Mrs. Kelly returned to take the girls into the conference room where the focus group meeting would be held, Meg was itching to give her opinions. So was everyone else. Mrs. Kelly had barely gotten them settled around the conference table and introduced them to the other grown-ups in the room, before they were making comments, giving suggestions, and tossing out ideas.

"What an enthusiastic group!" said the woman Mrs. Kelly had introduced as the product manager in charge of developing the games. She turned to a shy-looking young man with glasses who was sitting beside her. Pausing for a moment, as if to collect her thoughts, she said something to him that sounded sort of like what Brittany and her mother had been saying in the stationery store. The man responded with a rapid stream of words that left the product manager looking baffled.

Brittany, who'd been doodling on a notepad, looked up.

Uh-oh, Meg thought, here it comes. Don't be angry.

"*Parlez-vous français?*" said Brittany, a surprised expression on her face.

She must have said something about speaking French because the young man suddenly smiled. "Yes.

Oui," he said. Then he leaned across the table toward Brittany and began speaking eagerly in French.

"My goodness!" the manager exclaimed. "Janet, this is wonderful." She turned to Meg's mother. "You said you'd put together a great focus group for us, but I never dreamed you'd have someone who was able to speak French with Andre. Where did you find her?"

"I didn't find her. My daughter did," said Mrs. Kelly.

Meg wanted to disappear. She saw Cricket and Amy exchange a worried glance and felt Brittany's eyes upon her. What would Brittany do? Jump up and run from the room in tears? Accuse Meg of being a liar and a sneak? Meg wouldn't have blamed her one bit.

Instead, Brittany took a deep breath, as if to compose herself. Then she turned to the manager and said, "I'll be glad to help if I can. Please tell me what you want to say and I'll put it into French. He's been telling me that he has an idea for changing the design of the game so that—"

Meg couldn't listen. Even when the discussion finally moved from the programmer's problems to the ideas the girls had about the games, she felt like she was only half there. She heard Amy complain about the sea monsters moving too slowly in the submarine game that they'd played. She heard Cricket suggest they create a program for making paper dolls and printing them out. "Or maybe you could let kids design a whole doll house," she said. "There could be furniture and people and pets to put in. Kids could play around with it right there on the screen."

The product manager and the programmers nodded and scribbled notes and asked questions. Mrs. Kelly's boss was impressed. "This has been one of the most rewarding focus groups we've had. It's opened my eyes to a lot of possibilities," he said when the session was finally over. "You girls will each receive a check in the mail and you've certainly earned it. Thank you for your help."

Mrs. Kelly was beaming as they left the building and headed across the parking lot to the car. "You were great, girls!" she said. "Especially you, Brittany. We've all been stumbling along, trying to communicate with Andre in our high school French. He was so glad to have someone who could really understand him. And now," she went on, opening the car doors, "I'm going to treat you to hot fudge sundaes at Elmer's!" She herded the girls into the back seat, climbed in behind the steering wheel, and started the engine.

Meg could stand it no longer. "Brittany," she said, as her mother pulled out of the parking lot. "You've got to believe me. I never meant to—"

But Brittany didn't let her finish. "I know," she said. She reached across Cricket and Amy, who were sitting between them, and put her hand on Meg's arm. "And even if you did, what difference does it make? We're friends now. And this was such fun. Maybe we can do more things together, maybe even earn more money. I was thinking last night before I fell asleep that if we had a club . . ."

"Uh, Brittany," Cricket said, exchanging a glance with Amy and Meg. "I think there's something else we should tell you."

And when they got to Elmer's, they did.

It took a long time. Brittany and Amy kept making Meg and Cricket repeat things like how they'd found the attic and how they'd opened the footlocker.

"I can't wait to see the secret scrapbook," said Brittany. "To think that all this happened just because you were looking for—" She stopped. "You know what I'm going to do," she said suddenly. "I'm going to find a picture of myself when I was two years old and bring it in for the family bulletin board. If Mr. Crockett doesn't like it . . . well . . . it's just too bad!"

"That's a good idea," agreed Cricket. "And I don't think Mr. Crockett will mind. In fact I bet he'll rethink the assignment. There could be other kids who are having the same problem. But now . . ." She tapped on the table with her spoon. "I think we should take a vote. Do we want to have a club?"

"Of course we do!" exclaimed Amy. "We don't need to vote on it. We'll have our first meeting as soon as we get those checks. Then we can decide who gets to spend the money—one hundred dollars!" Her eyes lit up. "We can also decide who has to come up with the next project. It'll be just like your mothers' club. Agreed?"

Who could say no?

The hot fudge sundaes Meg's mother had ordered arrived at just that moment. And Mrs. Kelly herself—who'd disappeared after they sat down in the booth—reappeared, with a disposable camera in hand. "I got this at the shop next door," she said. "We can't let this moment go unrecorded. Now everyone, say cheese."

The girls leaned together, smiling behind their hot fudge sundaes, as she snapped a picture.

Meg reached into her pocket and pulled out Jenny's teddy bear. "Our mascot," she said, setting the silly little bear on the table. "He brought me luck finding all of you. Now he can bring all of us luck in the new Always Friends Club!"

Don't miss any of the great titles in the
ALWAYS FRIENDS CLUB series:

Meg and the Secret Scrapbook
0-8167-3578-6
$2.95 U.S./$3.95 CAN.

Cricket Goes to the Dogs
0-8167-3577-8
$2.95 U.S./$3.95 CAN.

Amy's Haunted House
0-8167-3576-X
$2.95 U.S./$3.95 CAN.

Beautiful Brittany
0-8167-3575-1
$2.95 U.S./$3.95 CAN.

Available wherever you buy books.